Praise For Eric J. Guignard

"Writing that captures the depth of emotion underlying fictional terrors."

—*Library Journal*

"Guignard's works are as shocking as they are thought-provoking."

—*Publishers Weekly*

"Eric J. Guignard is a talented author... his stories are beautifully written and compelling."

—*British Fantasy Society*

"Guignard gives voice to paranoid vision that's all too believable."

—Ramsey Campbell, Britain's most respected living horror writer (*Oxford Companion to English Literature*)

"For works that are beautiful and strange, read this writer of dark and speculative fiction!"

—*The Big Thrill Magazine*

"The defining new voice of horror has arrived!"

—Nancy Holder, NYT bestselling author, *Wicked*

"Guignard is someone to watch in horror."

—*Cemetery Dance Magazine*

"A helluva writer!"

—Rick Hautala, million-copy, international best-selling author of *Nightstone* and *Little Brothers*

"Eric J. Guignard crafts storytelling into timeless masterpieces… haunting stories that will captivate readers that relish dark fiction."

—*Fanbase Press*

"Guignard's writing is an adventurous journey the reader can think about long after the last page is turned."

—*Amazing Stories Magazine*

"Delivers fantastic tales… highly recommended."

—*Famous Monsters of Filmland*

"Eric J. Guignard is a visionary."

—Kaaron Warren, Multiple award-winning and best-selling author of *The Grief Hole* and *Slights*

"Guignard is highly recommended. Brilliant… deserves to be read."

—*Monster Librarian*

"When Eric J. Guignard's name is on something, it's like the Good Housekeeping Seal of Approval."

—Gene O'Neill, *Lethal Birds* and *The Cal Wild Chronicles*

Last Case at a Baggage Auction

Fiction Written by Eric J. Guignard

Doorways to the Deadeye (JournalStone, 2019)

Last Case at a Baggage Auction (Harper Day Books, 2020)

That Which Grows Wild: 16 Tales of Dark Fiction (Cemetery Dance Publications, 2018)

Anthologies Edited by Eric J. Guignard

A World of Horror (Dark Moon Books, 2018)

After Death... (Dark Moon Books, 2013)

Dark Tales of Lost Civilizations (Dark Moon Books, 2012)

The Five Senses of Horror (Dark Moon Books, 2018)

+Horror Library+ Volume 6 (Cutting Block Books/ Farolight Publishing, 2017)

Pop the Clutch: Thrilling Tales of Rockabilly, Monsters, and Hot Rod Horror (Dark Moon Books, 2019)

Exploring Dark Short Fiction (A Primer Series)
Created by Eric J. Guignard

#1: A Primer to Steve Rasnic Tem (Dark Moon Books, 2017)

#2: A Primer to Kaaron Warren (Dark Moon Books, 2018)

#3: A Primer to Nisi Shawl (Dark Moon Books, 2018)

#4: A Primer to Jeffrey Ford (Dark Moon Books, 2019)

#5: A Primer to Han Song (Dark Moon Books, 2020)

#6: A Primer to Ramsey Campbell (forthcoming) (Dark Moon Books, 2020)

The Horror Writers Association Presents:
Haunted Library of Horror Classics
Edited by Eric J. Guignard and Leslie S. Klinger

Vol. I: The Phantom of the Opera by Gaston Leroux (Sourcebooks, 2020)

Vol. II: The Beetle by Richard Marsh (Sourcebooks, 2020)

Vol. III: Vathek by William Beckford (Sourcebooks, 2020)

Vol. IV: The House on the Borderland by William Hope Hodgson (forthcoming) (Sourcebooks, 2020)

Vol. V: The Parasite and Other Tales of Terror by Arthur Conan Doyle (forthcoming) (Sourcebooks, 2021)

Vol. VI: The King in Yellow by Robert W. Chambers (forthcoming) (Sourcebooks, 2021)

Last Case at a Baggage Auction

By

Eric J. Guignard

With Illustrations by

Steve Lines

Harper Day Books
New York, NY

LAST CASE AT A BAGGAGE AUCTION

Interior layout by Eric J. Guignard
Cover design by Eric J. Guignard
www.ericjguignard.com

Front cover illustration by SessaV
www.instagram.com/sessav

Interior illustrations by Steve Lines
www.rainfallsite.com

Library of Congress Cataloging-in-Publication Data
Guignard, Eric J.
Last case at a baggage auction.

Library of Congress Control Number: 2020938951

First Harper Day Books editions
ISBN-13: 978-1-949491-25-8 (hardback)
ISBN-13: 978-1-949491-24-1 (paperback)
ISBN-13: 978-1-949491-26-5 (e-book)

First published by JournalStone in September, 2013
in variant text as "Baggage of Eternal Night"

HARPER DAY BOOKS
New York, NY

Made in the United States of America
(V071420)

Dedicated as always, and with love,
to my family—Jeannette, Julian, and Devin.

And to Lisa Morton for opportunity and support.

We're all collectors of something.

LES DEUX OIES
LES DEUX OIES

Table of Contents

-SL-
©2020

1.

I WANT TO tell you about Joey Third.

You probably never heard of Joey before, but at one time in the early 1950s he was a big-shot gambler in the underworld circles of Chicago and Detroit. Joey Thurston was his real name, but "Joey Third" is the name some wise guy called him on account of there being three different Joeys gambling one night in Little Louie's Den. After that, the name just stuck.

Joey and I became good friends. I didn't get to know him until after his poker days were over. I wouldn't have associated with him in those backroom circles anyway; those were the tables run by gangsters like Joseph Zerilli and Angelo Meli, men who could make you vanish if you laughed at the wrong joke or they didn't like the color of your tie. But by 1959, Joey had quit with the cards. Seemed that when he lost at poker, he really lost big. And when he won... well, he still lost. After a night of straight aces, two mucks accused him of cheating and they broke every bone in his left hand with a framing hammer. I don't believe Joey ever cheated—the times I knew him, he would return a gold watch to a man that dropped it on the street. I think those mucks that busted his hand were just sore losers. That, or their bosses were.

Anyway, how I met Joey was at the baggage auctions. Joey may have soured on cards, but he was a gambling man at heart. I began to recognize him at places like Roman's and the liquidation house on 23rd. I got used to seeing him waving that crippled hand of his up in the air, those ruined fingers askew like the twisted legs of a dead spider. Joey had an affable presence about him, a sense that, whether he was joking or irritable or even plain silent, one could still find companionship just by standing next to him. He was a genuine people-person. I won a few auctions over him, and he won a few over me, and pretty soon we'd get to drinking a couple mugs afterward, bearing a bond of baggage gambling.

Now, in case I'm getting ahead of myself, let me explain what a baggage auction is, for those of you not around during the war in the Koreas. These auctions are for pieces of luggage that go unclaimed at all the big hotels, pieces left inside the rooms. Maybe the guests forgot about their baggage. Maybe folks got locked up, or they didn't pay the bill... maybe they died. The bags are sold off unopened to the highest bidder. You never know what you're going to find inside, but with a little education and experience, you get pretty good at guessing. A big, frumpy carpet bag with paisley print on it likely contains some old marm's stockings and brassiere. A scuffed attaché case might contain makeup or the display merchandise of a traveling salesman. A midsize valise, plain in color, but from a high-end manufacturer—well, those are the best to go after. More often than not, you'll find a gentleman's vanity or lady's jewelry inside. The first time I competed in an auction, I bid one dollar and won a dented footlocker speckled on the front by dark stains. Inside was an envelope stuffed with ten fifty-dollar bills. After that, I was hooked for life.

The tale I want to tell you about Joey Third involves a leather suitcase he won at a baggage auction. I want to tell you about what was *inside* that suitcase.

It all began late on a Thursday afternoon in the midst of July. I remember that day because the Tigers had taken an awful pounding by the White Sox for three days in a row. The whole city just seemed to slump at that, as if every building and car were inflatable and air slowly leaked out from the seams. People were in a foul mood, and the summer heat didn't help none. The baggage auctions were normally a hoot for Joey and me both, but our hearts didn't seem to be in it that day.

The auctions were a weekly event, every Thursday afternoon, and that day it was held offsite in a distribution warehouse that doubled as a union hall. There weren't even chairs to sit on. We just stood in a large group, sweating and small-talking. Most of the guys in there knew each other—we all traveled to the same auctions the way you would follow horses at the tracks. We had our favorite auctioneers and our favorite hotels that the luggage came from. Today wasn't much different, except we were in the warehouse rather than a lodge or liquidation house.

Joey and I worked our way over to Ray Galler, a friend from the north side of town who owned a couple consignment shops. Ray was also an art and collectibles dealer who bought anything of value that we won. Between his stores and his private dealings, Ray could find a buyer for just about anything, if the price made sense. He was only a few years older than us but twice the hustler. I didn't make a lot of money from the auctions or races or my other gambling ventures—I also ghostwrote political editorials to pay the bills—but to Ray, the auctions were a way of life.

He had a habit of snapping his fingers when he spoke, as if the words hid a secret beat only he could hear. He snapped away. "Charlie, Joey, what do ya say? Anything lookin' hot?"

The bidding started at five o'clock, but you were allowed to preview the closed baggage for an hour before.

"Your eyes are as good as mine," Joey said.

"What do you think of the big steamer trunk over there?"

"I saw it," I replied. "Has nice locks, solid brass and polished. Somebody took good care of it."

"Could be some nice artwork inside," Ray said.

"Or Grandma's family photos," Joey replied. "Bet it wasn't used for nothing but a hope chest, filled with baby clothes."

"But why would someone cart it along to a hotel if that's all it held?" I asked.

"People bring strange things with them when they travel. You should know that by now."

Joey was right; I did know. The wonder was endless when it came to trinkets that people found valuable. I once knew a man who was destitute and homeless, but who carried with him a large box of baby rattles wherever he went. Those rattles meant the world to him, but to anyone else it was a collection of pastel-colored crap that sounded like shattering glass whenever he moved.

The auctioneer arrived and announced it was time to start bidding. Before you could whistle, the first suitcase was carried in by a porter and the auctioneer jumped right into the whole spiel. He was country-fat—the kind raised on gravy and hog—and his teeth stuck out as if his mouth caught fire and every chomper tried escaping in different directions. But his voice was molten honey, burning hot and pouring from between those screwy teeth in a flood of sweet words.

"First up open bid, one dollar for the green soft-case, do I hear one? One! Over there, do I hear two? Two! Over there, now three, give me three, three dollars for the soft-case. Three! The man in the back, going four, now four, do I hear four? Four! Man in the green coat, going five, now five, going five once, going five twice. Sold! Four dollars, man in the green coat."

The first case sold in about seven seconds, and one porter set it aside, while a second porter carried in the next item, a canvas tote bag.

As a matter of habit, Joey and I bid the minimum—one dollar—on just about anything, and the bids increased depending on our interest. The experienced bidders let the price rise on its own, as it didn't make sense to inflate the market right away on used items. That's how you could tell those who knew what they were doing against the dabblers, anyone who was anxious or inexperienced. Ten items into the auction, and one guy outbid everyone by yelling out forty bucks right away for a leather portmanteau. That suggested maybe it was his own to begin with and he needed it back. I used to think a sudden high bidder knew there was something valuable inside an item and tipped his hand the way a guy over-bets at cards when he's got a royal flush. I went up against a couple of those schleps in the past and won, only to find the case filled with stockings and rotting knickers. I lost a lot of money and couldn't get the smell from my nose for a week. You just never can figure out the motivation behind some people's bidding decisions.

As it was, we never did find out what was in that portmanteau, or if it was worth the money he over-bid. It was house policy—and common sense—that you opened the bags privately, off premises. There were two reasons for this: first, the auction houses didn't want winners to just skim the contents and leave the empty luggage lying around for the proprietor to have to dispose of. Second was for the safety of the winners; you didn't want to open a case in front of hoods when a trove of valuables might be stuffed inside.

That auction, Joey and I each won a couple of suitcases and purses. Just before we were set to leave and after the auction had ended, one of the porters ran up dragging a heavy leather case that had somehow been set apart from the others. The auctioneer announced there was another item, but most of the bidders were already leaving, and the rest had spent all their money. Joey won that last item with his default opening bid of one dollar.

Afterward, we went back to our apartments. Joey and I lived in the same building, me on the sixth floor and him on the fourth, of a complex that once had been a swanky hotel during the thirties, but since then changed owners and suffered renovations, so that linoleum and *Vacancy* placards overlaid the memory of its glitz. *Les Deux Oies*. That was its name—French for "The Two Geese." I'm told the hotel was originally owned by Hollywood Jews, designed by Swedes, built by Italians, and then christened in French. Maybe that's why it never succeeded: the national *melting pot* philosophy never seemed to fare well when it came to local business economy. Folks get confused, and a hotel ends up being called "The Two Geese."

We elected to go to my apartment, as it was filled with slightly less leftover luggage than Joey's. That's the burden of the auctions—we brought things in faster than we could dispose of them. Piles of teetering boxes and empty suitcases pressed up against the walls of our homes, nearly as high as the ceiling, placed where other men might erect bookcases or cabinets. Containers of shot glasses were stacked on cartons of bowling shoes that sat upon cases of screwdrivers that all listed precariously above egg crates filled with gloves and flashlights and tubes of artist's oil paints. Then, that was bookended on one side by the props from someone's Coney Island magic show and on the other side by a locker filled with the equipment of a man who scaled Mount Everest. Neighboring bulwarks were composed of magazines, German steins, fishing lures, candles, cufflinks, sports gear, batteries, bottle caps, typewriters with missing keys, ornamental Easter eggs, jars of face cream, wood carvings, cameras without film, and a thousand other items I meant to inventory but never got around to.

I brought out a couple of Stroh's beers, and Joey and me settled down on my living room floor to open what we won today.

It was like Christmas between us. We took turns opening each piece of luggage one-at-a-time, so as to share the excitement of its contents with each other.

"Lookee here, Charlie," he said as he popped the latches on a pink-striped carton. "I got a fancy evening gown. Maybe you have something I'll trade you for. This would make a nice gift for your lady friend to really impress her."

"Keep it. I've got a dozen in every color already stored in the back of my closet."

He laughed. "Yeah, I've got more broads' clothes than I do of my own. If anybody looked in my closet, they'd think I was a fruit."

I chuckled at that. Both our apartments looked like second-hand stores, filled with the junk of Detroit.

It was my turn, so I unlatched a valise, and looked inside. "Couple wigs in here to match your dress. A bunch of medications for stomach illness. Pair of Bibles. I suppose you need a backup in case the devil clips the first copy from you."

"The Gideons would be appreciative."

When you get to be middle-aged like we were, there're not a lot of thrills left in life, but opening the cases made us feel like excited children, exclaiming over what was inside. Sometimes we moaned over the contents, as a child does when finding a lump of coal in his stocking. Other times we shrieked with rapture, like the time Joey won a bid and found a stash of ruby-lined gold rings hidden inside, or when I found the polished old sword and pistol of a conquistador wrapped in gingham cloth at the bottom of a crate.

Today, it was mostly moans. Our other luggage held old men's shirts, dirty britches, hair tonic, and some nice shoes that were too large for either of us.

"Not even Ray's going to want any of this," I said. "I think we got skunked."

"Speak for yourself. I've still got that left-behind case I won last. It's old and heavy, and I'm feeling good about it." He held his hands over the case, as a mystic might do in order to discern its hidden power. "I'm hoping someone left bricks of gold inside."

Joey's last case *did* look old, and it looked European, like the kind of luggage shown on posters for luxury cruise liners that crossed the Atlantic. The large frame was wrapped in brown leather and crossed with a pair of double-stitched belts. Its handle appeared to have been carved from a hard, white substance like ivory, and there were similar white stones with a greenish hue embedded along the edge of the case where it would open apart.

"Never seen a piece of luggage like this," he said.

The suitcase was the size of two couch cushions stacked on top of each other and fastened by a thick bronze padlock overlaying the latches. "Don't suppose a key came with it?"

We owned a hammer and a set of chisels for breaking apart locked baggage. More often than not, however, we didn't need to use them. Joey maintained a collection of lock picks and the knowledge of how to use them. He selected a hook pick and twisted it around inside the lock for a few moments with his good hand. It clicked apart. Joey tossed the padlock aside and opened the case.

Inside was a gramophone, the old type of record player that was popular during turn-of-the-century years, with the horn speaker like a funnel that the sound came out from. I'd only seen units like that in the city museum and antique stores.

"Maybe we can invite some dolls over and have a party with this," he said.

I thought of my girlfriend Gail, who dressed nice and smelled good all the time and kept her home spotless. She hated coming over to visit me here. "Filthy," was the word she most frequently used to describe my living conditions.

"Gail's not too keen on carousing where stacks of boxes might topple onto her," I said.

"I didn't say *which* dolls to invite."

"Always causing trouble, ain't ya?"

Joey grinned. His lips pursed together and his cheeks rose, reminding me of a little boy who might suggest we sneak a sweet from the confectioner.

"Anyway, it probably doesn't work, it's so old," I said.

"And maybe it does," he replied. I couldn't tell if he was ribbing me or really *was* hoping to throw an impromptu bash. I hated people visiting whom I didn't already know. Gail was admittedly right in the description of my living conditions, and it embarrassed me.

Joey pulled the record player out and lifted the horn into place. The base of the player was rich-grained wood, sized about one foot in all dimensions. The turntable and horn were brass. A handle like the crank of an old car punched out from one side.

"I remember my grandmother used to have one of these in her sitting room," I said. "A real lively bird she was, playing music every afternoon, recorded by the pianist from her church."

"My grandma just whipped me with a stick of elm if the chickens weren't fed by sunrise."

"Is that why you're so damaged?"

Joey slapped me on the shoulder, and his chuckle made the room feel twice as large. "Here's cheers to grandmas, though I'd rather be cheering to some younger dames." He popped the cap off another Stroh's and downed half the bottle.

He continued. "I'll get this working and you'll either have a shindig with me, or I'll make you listen to piano gospel all night."

"Let's see what else you've got in there first."

Inside the old case were two more boxes, each with a flip lid, and I opened them.

Joey fingered through one. "Looks like there's quite a library of records in these boxes to mix it up. I suppose it's hoping too much for some Perry Como or The Shirelles."

Between the two boxes, I estimated there were about forty or fifty albums, each a flat black disc of wax. None of them were identified by labels, and each disc appeared identical: thick and handmade, with deep grooves set wider than the stereophonic vinyl albums of today.

"What do you make of this?" I asked and pointed at one of the boxes. A series of lines in strange writing like Eastern European characters were sketched in ink, followed by numbers, as if a series of ledger entries.

Joey set the gramophone on a chair and began winding the mechanical crank. Old record players worked like music boxes; the sound was produced through manual effort, without electrical amplification. "I don't know," he said, "but let's hear what they've got to say."

I pulled out a record, and Joey set it on the turntable. He released the crank. At first there was silence. I took another swig of Stroh's.

It started off with scratching sounds, like a hen trying to dig around in a yard made of sheet metal. Then some old-timey horn blew the most melancholy notes I ever heard, and that was followed by something that could have been a clarinet that played even more doleful than the horn. I heard a tinkling which might have been a piano and something else I couldn't even guess at, that sounded like someone with molasses in their throat breathing fast into a paper sack. If that was what music sounded like in the early nineteen hundreds, I understood why the country soon fell into a Depression.

"Makes me want to stab ice picks through my ears," Joey said.

The instruments played for half a minute in choral rhythm, following a series of timed beats and then crashed together in a burst of clatter, before slowing back down again. I once visited New Orleans in my younger days and heard the slow jazz marches of a funeral procession. If I had to make a comparison, this record sounded closest to that, only the instruments here were off-key and played together like children experimenting with contraptions found in the city dump.

And then a voice spoke.

Or, rather, chanted. Joey and I looked at each other. I immediately felt nauseous, the way castor oil curdles in your guts, and I saw Joey felt the same. The voice was a man's and he spoke in slow solemn words, the intonations seeming to reverberate throughout my room in low bass rumbles. The words were unfamiliar, but emotions dripping with wet fog somehow filled each syllable, and my head swooned.

Vkhodite. Vkhodite. Vkhodite.

Ne zaderzhivat'sya v kholodnyy i temnyy, ho prisoyedinit'sya ko mne v svet navsegda.

Vkhodite. Vkhodite. Vkhodite.

The impression changed and the nausea reversed until euphoria touched me. The words repeated over and over and each became a finger rubbing inside my temples, massaging my brain. The world seemed to shift slightly beneath me; shadows grew longer from behind the stacked baggage, and my thoughts slowed. I felt relaxed, like slipping under the water of a warm bath.

I lost track of time as the chanting words repeated themselves. I descended further into the bath sensation, floating free in a stillness that must be like what an embryo experiences as it develops in the womb.

Though I felt good, almost weightless, I sensed something was out of line.

"Turn it off," I finally said to Joey. He looked at me from far away, and his eyes were heavy-lidded, as I felt mine must have appeared to him. His expression though was wan as if he couldn't fathom who spoke, much less act on my directions.

I had to focus on the movements in my arm, but I willed myself forward. The record must have been playing for at least ten minutes, yet the needle still played in the first groove of the disc, as if it had only begun. I lifted the needle, and the sudden silence was like the slap of a cold hand.

Joey's eyes focused, and he leaned back to lie on the floor. "Mama, I feel like I just came off a three-day-bender."

"I feel like someone slugged me in the temple."

He rolled over and grinned. "Sure beats Grandma's church music."

I couldn't agree with that; I thought I'd rather listen to a hundred hours of piano hymnals than just a second more of that strange man's chant. His voice—those words—echoed in my mind.

Vkhodite. Vkhodite. Vkhodite...

The words were unfamiliar, yet they *spoke* to me. I couldn't understand them, but I believed it sounded like a modern language, if only some backward Baltic dialect. The speaker's articulation was flat, void of intonation, and the rhythm was like breathing. In fact, I felt that it somehow crept *inside* my breaths while I listened, the same way it climbed into my thoughts.

"Hey, Charlie, wake up." Joey snapped his fingers at me. "I said, 'What do you think the record was saying?'"

I looked at him, realizing part of me still drifted away. "I don't know, but it sure wasn't whispers of sweet love."

"Maybe this is some sort of hypnosis used on prisoners during the first World War. That'd make sense, right? I mean, if you wanted to drive someone crazy, just flick this on all night long."

"Maybe so," I said. "It bugged me out right away."

Joey nodded and we were quiet, each looking at the gramophone. If he were like me, Joey had to wonder at what exactly he brought home that night.

He lifted his crippled hand, looking at each finger one-by-one. "You know what else, Charlie?"

"I couldn't guess."

"I imagined I was flying," he said. "Does that make sense? While that played, I felt like my body didn't weigh anything and I lifted from the earth. I mean, I knew it was wrong, but I couldn't control it. I just drifted up into the stars."

"Funny," I said. "I kind of felt the same, like I was floating free in a warm bath."

"What do you think these records are worth?"

"A trip to the city dump."

"Get outta here! I've never encountered anything like this before. That's got to account for something. You think Ray will take a look at it?"

"Maybe. Or maybe we should just scrap the thing. We seem to agree there's something off about it."

Joey either ignored my comment or wasn't listening. "Ray

knows antiques. Of course, this being a foreign language might throw him. I sure wish I knew what it said."

"Aw, hell, I know a guy who's into languages." I said. I thought Joey was probably right about it having some sort of value. Of course, when it came down to it, the weirder an item, the more value it commands. "Real sharp fella, this guy. He's a Hungarian that runs a book store I used to live by, about as cultured a mind as you're going to find in these parts. I'll bring him the record player in the morning and ask what he makes of it."

"Leave the player. Just bring him a couple of the albums. I'm going to listen to some of the others on my own, see what else is on here."

"What's he going to do with records and no player to put them on?"

"It's 1963. Everyone's got a record player."

I shrugged, and Joey packed up the gramophone and his other winning baggage. We said our goodnights, and he walked out the door of my apartment. As soon as he left, the room felt a little colder, a little smaller.

1963 was half over and I felt old and slow, as if the year sped past, shooting clouds of dust at me as it blew by. I remembered that I once had a plan for life, a direction, but now I just lived for the day. Making bets and going to the auctions was always a hoot, but part of me felt that I settled for something I wasn't meant for. Truth was, I always wanted to live in the city, but I also thought I would get a fancy job in business or law, drive a big car, and travel to Europe. I made it to the city, but I found regular work didn't suit me. Getting chained to a desk for ten hours a day made me think of stories about men who drowned in quicksand:

once they start sinking, it's harder and harder to get out, and after a certain threshold is passed—just above the naval on a full-grown man—escape is impossible. They can only scream and flounder and know death is cruel and inevitable. To me, that's what every day at an office job was like.

I got out in time, but I also lost my dream. I might have given up and moved back to the warmer climes of my native Kentucky, if I hadn't then met my ex, Danielle. She and I had got engaged quick, ten years ago, and life had sure gotten rosier, until I caught her in bed with a jockey... a jockey I had bet against earlier that day at the track and who went against the odds, winning in the final lap! Within five hours, I lost my money and I lost *her*. I stood a foot taller than that horse-riding bastard, and when I caught them doing the wild mamba in bed I called him out and laid all my force into a crack against his jaw. He barely flinched, and then he landed an uppercut that knocked me clean out. When I woke, they both were gone. To this day, all I can figure is that he was experienced with having wronged men hit him and had trained to take punches.

Either that, or I hit like a pansy.

After Danielle, I met Gail, whom I've come to love like no other. If not for what happened with Danielle, I would have proposed marriage to Gail long ago. As it was, I couldn't bring myself to do it again. Too much pain and betrayal associated with the custom. Gail kept me rooted in reality; she worked the regular business job I couldn't hold, she had the big car and the future. I wished someday to make an honest woman out of her, though I knew deep down she deserved better than me. I regularly expected her to cut me loose.

How many Stroh's did I drink? I thought of Joey and Danielle and Gail and all the people from my life speaking to me from a record. And there, tiny amongst the towers of luggage and reminiscences, I faded into night's dreams.

-SL-
©2020

2.

THE NEXT DAY I drove to Vic's Books in one of the city's historic quarters lining the Detroit River's north bank. Vic was west of the Ambassador Bridge that connects to Canada, and every time I drove past, I thought of how many forlorn people took a quarter mile walk either way, hoping to start life over in a new country, only to find out that it's the same troubles everywhere.

I arrived at the shop and parked in front. Vic's Books was a small glass-faced square in the shopping district, one of many like an assemblage of bright children's blocks laid in line.

Carrying three of Joey's records wrapped in a pillowcase, I pushed through the front door. A small bell announced my entrance. Inside were cases of paperbacks and clothbound volumes crammed into every space. The musty smell of aged paper filled the room like a presence—a good presence—and I was reminded of lazy afternoons lounging in my grandfather's study reading childhood adventures in exotic lands.

There were no other customers in the store, and I made my way through towering aisles of ancient tomes and Harlequin tales until I reached the back, where Vic sat reading the *Detroit Times* and smoking a frayed cigar.

"Charlie," he said without looking up. "Been too long since you stopped by. Never be too busy to read, son."

"I read."

"The pony stats don't count." He looked at me over the edge of gold-rimmed focals, the kind with a piece of twine that circles your head and attaches to the arms like a necklace.

"All right, I'll buy something if that's what you want," I said.

"Of course that's what I want. I run a business don't I?"

"I said I'll buy something." I shrugged.

He shrugged back.

"And it's nice to see you, too," I added.

"Hey, I'm just giving you a hard time."

"Same old Vic. You age, you don't change."

He smiled at that, and a gleam shone from the edge of one silver tooth. "I want to be mythified."

"I have a favor to ask," I said.

Vic folded the paper and scratched at his gray whiskers. "As long as it don't involve money or lipstick."

"Not sure what it involves, but probably only a few minutes of reaching back to your homeland." I laid the records on the counter next to him.

"You want me to listen to music?"

"A pal procured these in an old traveler's suitcase. The records are of someone chanting—real eerie stuff. And they don't play right either, like the grooves in the wax are stretched or extended somehow. The records seem to run longer than they should, as if they won't end." I looked at Vic to make sure he didn't think I was cracked. He just nodded, so I continued. "Anyway, I think it's an Eastern European language, Baltic origins or something. Lot of 'V' and 'Z' sounds. We want to know what they're saying in the chants and maybe if there's some value here. Who better to turn to than my old Hungarian pal in the antiquities market, eh?" I smiled, though maybe a bit too much.

"Sounds curious," he replied. "But I don't have a record player."

I laughed inwardly, wishing Joey was there.

"I'll pass it around to someone else I know," Vic added. "These discs look handmade, so you never know what's recorded on them. Probably nothing more than a family choir recital. Come back in a week—next Friday morning—and I'll let you know what I find out."

"Thanks, Vic."

"Don't think about it." He puffed on his cigar and looked around. "Now buy something, would ya? The store don't run on my favors."

Not feeling any great inspiration, I picked up a couple science fiction paperbacks showing covers of green-skinned aliens and spacecraft that looked like flying dinner plates.

When I got home, I tossed the books into a box with a hundred other paperbacks I would probably never read. Besides clothes and makeup, used books were the most common item I found inside baggage. It seemed nearly everyone carried a book about mystery or adventure or advice when they traveled.

I farted around for the next few days, talked with Gail on the phone each evening, and made plans to accompany her and her boss to dinner on Tuesday at Frantillo's. I always enjoyed chatting with Gail; the day didn't seem properly lived if I didn't cap it off with her spirited conversation.

Anyway, that date at Frantillo's wasn't until midweek, so I should have had plenty of time to prepare. Of course, Tuesday afternoon arrived sooner than expected, and I found myself scrambling at the eleventh hour to make her schedule.

Don't be late, Gail had said. *You're always running behind, so leave early if you have to. Be here at five thirty. It's my boss, Geoff Van Duyn, and his wife. Don't make me look bad.*

Her words rang in my head when I ran into Joey in the lobby of Les Deux Oies. I had just bought a bouquet of calla lilies for Gail from the corner vendor and was rushing back to my room to change into dinner clothes.

Joey came out of the elevator when I was about to go up. He looked peculiar somehow, messy in a way that was antithesis to his customary care in grooming: polished shoes, oiled hair, shirts pressed so tight that finding a wrinkle was like searching for fins on a pigeon. Now he was pale, and I guessed he hadn't shaved since last I saw him.

"Joey," I said. "You okay? You look terrible."

"Sorry, Charlie. I didn't know I had to impress anyone today."

"Fair enough. Suppose I did put my foot in my mouth."

"Don't worry about it." He paused, holding the elevator open for me. "Going up, or am I holding the doors 'cause I got nothing else to do?"

Sometimes when Joey spoke, I couldn't tell if he was wisecracking or in a pissy mood. I got the feeling today was the latter case.

"I've got a few minutes. Why don't I walk with you?"

"Suit yourself." He let the doors close, and we passed through the lobby.

"Find anything new on those records?" I asked.

He seemed to flinch slightly and walked a step faster.

"I've been listening to them every day," he finally said. "But I still don't know what any of it means. They're all the same, by the way. Every record is the same, 'cept I've noticed one thing."

"What's that?"

We reached the glass doors that led outside to the street, and just before pushing through, he stopped. Joey glanced around as if making sure nobody could overhear him, and his voice lowered.

"After that first voice chants for awhile, a second voice joins in, repeating the words of the first voice. But the second voice is different on each album. Some are a man's and some are a woman's, some sound old and some young. They're different people joining in, but, otherwise, the records are the same. That god-awful music and the creepy chant. *Vkhodite. Vkhodite. Vkhodite.* I never heard of such a thing."

"Do you... " I started to say, then stuttered, not sure how to phrase the question. "When it's playing, do you still feel the same, like what happened in my apartment?"

He nodded, and his voice lowered even more.

"It's strange, Charlie. Even when I'm not listening to a record, the music keeps playing in my head. It's like it won't turn off. But I don't want it to turn off, either. It makes me feel good, like it's *supposed* to be playing, like it's sharing a great secret."

"Maybe you shouldn't play it for awhile. You said before, it could be some sort of hypnosis. Who knows what's it's doing—could be rewriting your brain. Turn it off until we figure out what it is."

"But that's just it," he said. "I think the records are telling me something. They *want* me to know. I'm not saying the music is swingin' good times—it's pretty wretched sounds—but it changes as you listen. It causes you to visualize things. I see a clearing in a forest that's covered in snow. I see a faraway castle with turrets that look like Christmas tree ornaments. The records are preparing me... a new life, away from pain and fear."

Joey's eyes seemed to glaze over.

"That sounds pretty cracked to me," I said.

Maybe I shouldn't have been so blunt in my response. He startled, and a dark shadow passed over his face. I wondered later if I would have nodded some understanding and inquired further, Joey might have opened up a bit more. He might have told me *who* he saw in his visions, what he expected, and what was told to him.

Instead, he clammed up. "Yeah, you're right. It's crazy talk. I've got to go anyway. You're not going to follow me around all day are you?"

"I've got my own plans."

"Good seeing you, Charlie."

"We still on for Roman's auction this Thursday?" I asked, as Joey pushed through the doors to exit.

"Wouldn't miss it," he replied and was gone in a blink.

My side venture with Joey took no more than fifteen minutes. But by the time I went up to my room, dressed for dinner, searched for my car keys (somehow fallen behind the wood locker of a ventriloquist dummy), returned back downstairs, and drove across the city to meet Gail, I was mortified to see that time had skipped forward in a hurry. My watch read five forty-five.

The parking lot at Frantillo's was filled, so I went around the corner to find a space for my car. I fast-walked back to the restaurant feeling every second ticking away in my head. Frantillo's was a small joint, low-roofed and snazzy with big windows covered by thick crimson blinds. The afternoon sun still hung high, and it played funny tricks in the reflections of the glass. I imagined Gail looking out at me from behind the curtains in disappointment.

Inside, the maître d' barely looked up before asking if I had a reservation. I'm sure he thought I was riffraff. He smelled of cheap aftershave and French cheese.

"I'm expected," I said. I walked past, and he shook his head as if I were lying.

The bar area was packed with young businessmen decked out in wide-lapel suits and shoes so shiny it was like walking past a row of mirrors. Everyone in there could have been part of a collection of animatrons: they looked the same, laughed the same, talked about the same topics. *Business meetings, business clients, business opportunities.* It was a world I despised. Maybe I loathed it because I had once tried to fit in, only to flounder helplessly instead. Failure rears resentment.

I don't know why I let it bother me; I was as happy with life as I deserved and should only wish the same for everyone else. I passed into the dining room, which was arranged in a maze of high-backed booths allowing privacy to each party from surrounding patrons. The lighting was dim, and Italian ballads drifted over muted conversations. I zigzagged through until I found Gail. She sat by herself at a table set with three half-drunk glasses of red wine.

"Hi." I waved. "Sorry I'm late, dear. Only by fifteen minutes this time."

"Try twenty." She got up to meet me, wearing a tight shirtwaist dress with big black buttons that looked ready to pop off. Though she was a few years older than me, Gail could doll herself up to look half her age. She was a full-sized woman with curves like a pair of necking swans.

"Twenty's not so bad." I leaned in for a smooch.

She pulled away. "Twenty today, thirty yesterday, an hour tomorrow. When are you going to win a working clock at one of your auctions?"

"Brought you something," I said and handed her the calla lilies I'd been carrying since the apartments. "Won't you feel bad for scolding when I explain how I scoured the florists of Detroit, handpicking only the finest of lilies for your pleasure?"

"I might, if it were the truth," she said.

Gail accepted the flowers, and my charm won over her scowl. She smiled, and we kissed.

"Did I miss much?" I asked.

"Geoff's mingling at the bar. He saw some buddies from a club—either polo or yachting or men of inherited fortune—and went over to show off his wife. She's nineteen years younger than him, you know. Took their second honeymoon last month."

I rolled my eyes. "I sure fit in."

"You can *try* to make me look good. He's heading up store expansion in the New England markets, and I'm in the running for a promotion. A woman with a man does better climbing the corporate ladder than a woman without." Her voice turned confidential. "You know how much trouble we get into if left to our own devices."

She pinched the inside of my thigh and winked.

I startled, and a tiny squeal slipped out. "You jezebel!" I pinched her back.

She never pressured me over it, but I knew in those years it was true, that a married woman was looked upon more favorably than an unmarried one, at least in terms of the business world. Gail even wore a small diamond ring on her wedding finger that I gave her some years back. It wasn't an engagement ring or promise ring or anything sentimental, just something I won inside a satchel at a baggage auction and gifted her to make up after an argument. But it served a purpose also, as long as nobody asked too many questions.

"So how are you?" she asked. "Busy day in the junk trade?"

"I made a few dollars."

"Enough to take me to dinner next week? Just you and me, maybe a night of dancing at Morton's Jazz Club?"

"I think that could be arranged."

She ran a finger along the back of my hand. "We don't get out enough, Charlie. It's always nice just to be with you."

"Agreed," I said. "Maybe we can get together this weekend."

Gail nodded as Geoff Van Duyn and his wife returned to the table.

I sighed inwardly. Van Duyn looked as if every businessman I had passed at the bar were rolled up into one mega-agency man. Though I'd never met him, I knew much about Van Duyn through conversations with Gail in which she'd recite each workday's highs and lows, her projects and aspirations and office gossip. I knew he liked theater but not sporting events, yachts but not planes, stocks but not bonds. Van Duyn liked his coffee black, his ties red, and his wives blonde.

Gail worked in the corporate office for Rockwell's department stores, a chain of high-end retailers that carried everything a modern family could want, from clothes to bedding to appliances to toys. She managed procurement for designer women's clothes, some of it pretty hoity-toity fashion. I needled her whenever I won a piece of luggage with Rockwell's dresses tucked inside; everything became "second-hand" eventually. I purchased things for pennies of what she sold on the racks.

Van Duyn was Vice President of purchasing. He was her boss and, as such, determined her future with the company.

Introductions were made, and he started right in on me.

"You a businessman, Charlie?"

"I'm self-employed."

"No kidding. A self-made man?"

"A man still in the making," I said.

He guffawed like a cat choking up a hairball. "Funny stuff." He turned to Gail. "You didn't tell me he had a sense of humor."

"That's Charlie," she said, and I could sense the nervousness in her voice.

"So what is it you do?" Van Duyn asked.

"I'm involved in a few different ventures. I write editorials and buy and sell collectibles."

"Sounds like hobbies, not an occupation."

"I control my own destiny," I said, cringing at the slip of cliché.

"I'll give you that," he replied. "But why knock yourself out, scrambling for pennies? Get a real job, I say, so you have security and can share life's luxuries with Gail."

I had it pre-rehearsed. "A man is successful if he lives every day with the ability to do what he wants."

Van Duyn nodded, expecting me to continue. I didn't have any more to say on the subject, but they were all looking at me and the silence grew awkward fast. I grasped for something else to add that would seem important.

"*Um*, our time on Earth is limited, and there's no point wasting it living someone else's life. Every man's vision of triumph is different, and the truest measure is how honest you are with yourself. Pursue your passion, and success will follow."

What I'd said sounded so sincere and knowledgeable I wished I'd written it down for future use, though I didn't think I could repeat it again with a straight face. It was probably just recollection of some jumbled phrases from old management pep-talks, back when I *was* in business. But the others nodded and agreed, commenting on the wisdom I'd shared. Van Duyn said if I ever wanted to try my hand in the department store business, he'd have a job for me. A waiter arrived to take our order, and afterward the conversation changed to lighter topics.

I can't say the rest of the evening was pleasant, but it was more bearable than I'd expected.

-SL-
©2020

3.

THE NEXT COUPLE days passed as if they didn't exist. I felt antsy like there was something I was supposed to do, or else I was missing an affair, the way a celebration occurs and you show up at two in the morning after it's ended. By the time you arrive, everyone is passed-out drunk, and the music's turned off, and the pink streamers hanging off light fixtures just look limp and spent. During that time I penned some editorials and nursed a steady, dull ache in my head. I sold some collectible spoons to a silver dealer and wrote a monthly letter to my folks back home. Each night I dreamt of people sitting around a campfire in the snow, like a powwow. Around them spread a forest, and I wondered if it was the same snowy forest that Joey said he dreamt of. The people sitting around the campfire had empty faces, each just the shell of an egg sitting on top of a torso, and they disappeared into the night one-by-one.

By the time Thursday afternoon arrived, I was bored and desperate for some action. I'd been waiting for today's baggage auction for a long time; I hadn't been to an auction or race in a week, as all the tracks were closed for the summer heat and most other "venues of chance" were on hiatus. I ironed my pants and dialed Joey at the same time, holding the handset in the crook of my neck while steam drifted up my face.

He picked up after nine rings.

"Hey, it's me, Charlie. You ready? Roman's is opening in half an hour. Want me to meet at your room?"

"Charlie… ?" His voice drifted, as if my name were a question or a fleeting memory from something long ago.

"Yeah, from upstairs. You drinkin' already?"

There was a pause between us, and in that lack of conversation I heard dim voices in the background, muffled by distant music, but words repeating, chanting.

The records.

"Hey, pal," he said slowly. "I'm not feeling up to snuff today. Why don't you go on without me."

"Geez, they're liquidating baggage from the Lincolnwood Hyatt today. The Lincolnwood! Kim Novak roosted there last month, vacationing from Hollywood. I heard the porter lost one of her satchels. Who knows what might turn up today."

"Make a bid for me. I'm gonna take it easy."

"You want me to pick up some soup for you on the way back?"

"No, no, pal, it's okay. I'm just gonna sleep it off."

I shrugged, as if he could see me through the phone line. "Okay, hope you feel better tomorrow."

"Thanks," he replied. "We'll be fine."

"Who's 'we'?" I asked, but the line went dead as he hung up.

I never knew Joey to call off plans due to sickness. Catching the sniffles wasn't reason enough to skip playing the auctions. Of course, age *was* catching up to us, and the weather extremes didn't help. As of late, I also had felt sluggish, my mind a bit muddled. Maybe there was a bug going around the hotel. Now that I thought about it, that wouldn't surprise me at all. Who knew what kind of foul things died in the ducts, their carcasses left rotting so the gases of death bubbled out from the hissing vents into our rooms. Les Deux Oies wasn't exactly a sanctuary of sanitation; I'd seen mold in the halls and roaches scurrying into ever-widening cracks. Not a lot, mind you, but their occasional appearances were just enough to remind you that things causing the willies existed all around and there wasn't much you could do about it. I had spoken to the building's superintendent, Horace Wetzel, about the declining condition, but he just nodded and said he'd check it out, all the while giving me that look: *If you don't like it, you can go somewhere else.*

So I did, at least for the evening. I went to Roman's.

By the time I arrived, the auction house was filled with gamblers, investors, goons, and degenerates. It reminded me of a scene from an old James Cagney mobster movie. Groups of men dressed in shiny suits stood around, their eyes hidden in the shadows of low-slung fedoras, and they all turned to me as I walked through the front entrance.

"Charlie, over here," Ray Galler called out. He stood with a couple of bespectacled men who were built skinny and narrow-faced like accountants. "This is John A. and John T." He tilted his head at me. "Johns, this is Charlie Stewart."

"Did you hear Kim Novak's satchel is supposed to be here?" one of the Johns asked.

"Knew since it went missing," I replied with a wink.

"This is the Johns' first time at the auctions. I'm training them to run my stores, and I told them you're one of the smartest bidders to watch," Ray said. He looked past me. "Where's Joey?"

"Took a sick day. Too much sun."

"Huh. Not like him to miss out on something like the Lincolnwood."

"Don't I know it. But what can you do if health deals you a bum hand for the day? Take it and reshuffle tomorrow."

"One less bidder sounds fine by me," the other John said.

I was going to snap something back, real witty, too, but the auctioneer started in on his spiel.

I had twenty bucks in my pocket and was itching to spend it. The first case went up: a caramel-colored piece of luggage with a saddle belt wrapped around each side. I bid my opening dollar and Ray went to two. The dollars increased until Ray won at six and a half. The next item was a checkered satchel. Ray won that, too. An hour later, I still had twenty bucks in my pocket.

I'd been outbid on everything, most noticeably by Ray and the accountants. They must have bought at least three-quarters of the luggage so far.

"What gives?" I whispered to him. "You've spent half the economy of Detroit. You know something I don't?"

"Feeling lucky today, Charlie. It's more than Kim Novak who's stayed at the Lincolnwood lately."

That did it. I'd been moping around all week, and I refused to go home empty-handed now. The next item the auctioneer called out was a leather suitcase, its face more cracked than a smiling politician. The edges were frayed and the locks shed flecks of rust.

"Opening bid, do I hear an opening bid for this fine gentleman's case?" said the auctioneer.

"One dollar," Ray said.

"One dollar over there, do I hear two?"

"Ten," I called out.

The auctioneer coughed.

I hated myself. I knew it was a bad bid, a *dabbler* move,

but the craving to win had hold. Buyer's remorse was nothing compared with the hasty impulse to make an offer on an item, knowing the auction was soon-to-close; I came all the way down here and I *had* to gamble on something.

"Ten dollars, the man with the big wallet. Now ten, going eleven, going eleven once, going eleven twice. Sold! Ten dollars."

"I wouldn't have gone past two," Ray whispered.

"Sometimes it takes a little jolt to get into the action," I said.

"The action's all gone, buddy. There's only one more case left."

A porter carried out a busted suitcase held together by bailing twine.

"Last item," called the auctioneer. "A promising treasure trove, this case is bursting with potential. Do I hear an opening bid?"

Ah, to Hell with it, I thought.

"Ten dollars," I shouted.

I heard the crowd collectively groan.

Later, as we collected our winnings, Ray approached and slapped me on the back.

"Tough bids," he said, snapping his fingers.

"Just like playin' ball. Some games you're a star, and others you wish you never signed up. Maybe Joey was onto something staying home today."

"Who knows, you could find the Queen's Diamond hidden inside."

"Not in these dogs." We both knew I'd been a dummy.

"Listen, the reason I'm bringing the Johns into my business is that I want to spend more time hunting for the *real finds,* peoples' heirlooms and found artifacts. The baggage auctions are great, but I'm fixing on attending antique show circuits and estate sales, connecting with property liquidators and dealers."

"Branching out? There's no one better finding value in the throwaway trade."

"It's all part of a grand plan," he said. The two accountants appeared on either side of him like a pair of guard dogs. "Acquisitions is the key."

The crowd was thinning, bidders making their way to cars waiting outside. Most of the auction attendees were suspicious of everyone else and guarded their wins the way misers watch pennies. I always thought it was guilt that gnawed at men like that; those who stole before were most likely now to distrust the world around them.

I turned back to Ray with the mountain of cases piled around him. He must have bought at least fifty items. "So what do you want? A hand carrying out your winnings?"

He snorted. He snapped his fingers. "I want to see your apartment, Charlie. You and Joey bring some top finds to me. What do you do with the rest of your winnings, the loafers and perfumes and broken toys that most of us cart home like we're the city garbage men?" He toed my case, the one held together by twine.

"It keeps me company at night," I said.

Ray snorted again. Snapped again. "I've been trading collectibles a lot longer than you. Let me take a look at what else you've got. I may find some things in your home with value you don't know about. I could take 'em off your hands."

He was offering to cart out some of my junk *and* pay me? I asked, "Tomorrow afternoon soon enough?"

"I'll be there at three."

I wished him luck for the rest of the night and went out the door.

The trip back to Les Deux Oies was slow-going. I had a Ford and I babied her. She was a powder-blue Crestline, '52 model, lot of miles and a lot of good memories. But she was ailing now, the transmission gears starting to slip and alignment pulling to the right. I'd just replaced a cracked windshield and blown muffler, and I knew some expensive repairs were in my future. I cussed myself out that I'd gotten caught up in the bids and blew through a twenty for no good reason.

Back in the apartments, a funny thing happened. I was going up the rickety elevator, suitcases in hand, along with a man I recognized as Joey's neighbor, Martin something-or-other. I didn't particularly know him, though we'd been introduced in passing a year or two ago. He was young and blond, some sort of Scandinavian stock, and married to a gorgeous dame who could have passed for his sister.

"Evening," I said and nodded a greeting at him.

He returned the sentiment.

As we arrived at the fourth floor, I felt a tug in my mind, like a cartoon-hand aroma tickling my senses, enticing me to get off and follow its lead. The doors parted, and Martin stepped out, muttering, "*Vkhodite.*"

"Excuse me?"

He didn't respond, just hurried away, vanishing behind the closing doors. The elevator rose, and the cartoon-hand aroma sensation passed, but I felt the aftereffect; that tingling when you know you've narrowly missed something bad, the out-of-control truck coming right at you, and—just when you brace yourself to be hit—it corrects itself and drives away. I sensed it was Joey's room calling me, and my gut instinct said to stay away. My gut instinct said to never go down to that fourth floor again.

By the time I settled in for the evening, I'd tossed back two Stroh's beers and set a third on top of a hope chest that once belonged to a woman whose son helped build the Empire State Building. I knew, because inside were photo albums of him wearing suspenders and a flat cap in all manner of poses along the timeline of its construction. I thought often of the photos I possessed of other people's lives, people I didn't know but whose memories I kept stashed under trunk lids. Were these people all dead now? Did they have families who wondered whatever happened to pictures and mementoes passed down from generation to generation until, one day, such remembrances simply absconded into the unknown?

The cases I won were left open on the floor where I'd dumped their contents. I'd spent twenty bucks and lugged home a pair of four-foot paperweights, for all the worth they held. The first case with the cracked face was stuffed with wrinkled children's clothes, and the busted second case contained paperwork relating to a dairy business proposal. I did find one item of interest, hidden under a false bottom beneath the kids' clothes: a nudie magazine from 1939. I thumbed through it and mused that these were simply more photographs of other people's lives come into my possession.

As the deep-sea shadows of night rolled in, I found myself contemplative again of life, and the "what if" questions flicked through my thoughts. *What if* I had stayed with my family out in the Kentucky wheatlands, where the sun shone across a wide blue sky like molten gold. Maybe I'd be a hayseed farmer, plowing Poppa's fields and spending afternoons fishing in the Blueway River with little care in the world. *What if* I forgave Danielle, the woman I was engaged to a decade ago, who cheated on me with the jockey? Maybe we'd be settled now with a couple of children, living in a cottage down by the lakeshore. *What if* I never met Danielle? Maybe I'd be more open with Gail, more trusting to tend my feelings with her... I'm sure I would have proposed marriage by now. *What if* I had managed to keep a "real" profession, accounting or insurance, something stable where I could surrender to those long hours but feel the elusive hope of "security"? I thought I'd be dead from a heart attack. *What if* Momma and Poppa were right? *Nothing good ever comes from moving to the city. What if, what if, what if...*

The world turned off, a television show that cuts away to a black screen. Maybe the channels turned, for I was taken to slumber, and, in dreams, saw again the faceless people in the winter forest. There were perhaps forty or fifty men and women settled around an enormous campfire. I felt alone, cold and adrift, and I wanted to join them. At that thought, a blurry figure rose from their assemblage, arms open in welcome. He possessed no real form, no features, just a sense of flowing robes and ethereal limbs. Through him, *inside him*, I saw the universe twinkling like the floating embers.

Come in, he said. *Come in from the cold.*

And I wanted to join them, that group settled in trance around the flames. But I knew, too, I would give up something if I did, something I held dear, some part of myself. I fought the urge to move closer.

The figure's voice became angry. *Come in, or I will take you...*

-SL-
©2020

4.

THE NEXT MORNING was Friday. I brushed aside remnants of the strange dream and made chicken soup and fried some eggs for breakfast. I cooked an extra portion and brought it down to Joey's apartment.

I heard the record playing halfway down the hall before I reached his room. The walls were thin as a weekday newspaper, and I wondered that his neighbors didn't complain. How long had the chanting songs been going on for? All night, or did he wake up and start playing them when he rolled out of bed? I wondered, too, how far echoes of that music could drift.

"Hey, Joey," I called out and knocked on his door.

No answer. I pounded several times until a woman across the hall opened her door. She had blue hair from a bad dye job, wrapped in pink curlers to make it look even worse.

"You playin' a conga over there?" she said.

"Sorry," I muttered.

I had a key to Joey's place, but I knew not to use it unless it was prearranged or an emergency. We both kept keys to each others' apartments in cases of turning off the gas or bringing in the mail if one of us was away for awhile. I didn't think today would constitute an emergency, but I knew, too, that he'd been real sick.

I let myself into Joey's room and closed the door behind.

His apartment looked as if an earthquake had struck, knocking all his belongings down, and then cleaned up by a tornado, tossing them into great heaps. There were luggage and collectibles filling the room, mirroring my own apartment, but thrown in teetering piles against the walls rather than stacked and organized. Normally he was like me, a sucker for collecting, but also tidy, keeping the place in a livable condition. It seemed now that he'd just shoved everything aside in order to have one large, empty area in the middle of the living room.

That's where I found him, listening to the record player, sitting on the floor in a sort of trance, and chanting along with the strange musical words.

Vkhodite. Vkhodite. Vkhodite.

Ne zaderzhivat'sya v kholodnyy i temnyy, ho prisoyedinit'sya ko mne v svet navsegda.

"You alive in here?" I asked. "Didn't you hear me knocking?"

No response. He kept chanting, and I noticed his body swayed slightly, rocking back and forth.

I stepped closer to him. "Joey!"

At the same time, he stopped chanting and turned to me, and I saw a flash of movement in my peripheral vision. I tried to look in two separate directions: in one, I saw Joey looking sicker than ever, his eyes milky and skin pale-blue, and in the other direction the after-image of a figure that vanished, a wild-bearded man in flowing robes. I tried to exclaim at both simultaneously.

"God, Joey, are you okay?" and "Who else is in here?"

I was so taken aback, though, my words mixed and came out instead as an incomprehensible babble: "*God—who—Joey—else—you—in here!*"

"Charlie, you all right?" he finally said.

"Me? Who's asking? The guy that looks like he's been drowned for three days? I've never seen someone pale as a dead fish before."

"I look like that?"

"Yeah, pretty much." Then I rephrased the *other* first question I had tried to ask. "Who else is here?"

"No one but us chickens."

"There was a man, with crazy hair and a beard, like he hadn't shaved in a century."

Joey's mouth fell open, and I could see, even from a distance, he hadn't brushed his teeth in a long time. "You saw him?"

"So there *is* someone?"

"I don't know. I was dreaming of snow and sky... the bearded man was leading me through, so I wouldn't get lost."

"Don't get nutty." I turned and called across the apartment toward the bed and bathroom. "Hello? Come on out."

"No, Charlie, he ain't here. You just saw my dream, is all."

The record was still playing, that cacophony of crashing instruments and solemn words repeating its strange invocation. I felt dizzy, yet ethereal at the same time, like if I fell I would slip *up* an inverted slope, lifted by a reversal of gravity.

"Turn that crap off!" I yelled. Even when I said those words, though, part of me wanted to settle down on the floor right next to Joey. I sensed a great revelation forming, a secret gift offered if only I would listen to the record. But, more than that, I just felt flustered and confused, the way a dream twists your perception.

Joey moved in slow-motion, still seeming to sway back-and-forth. He tilted his head as if trying to comprehend my request, and I saw the quarrel in his eyes, the internal dispute as part of him demanded to let the music continue playing. Maybe he was worn down, or maybe he obliged for my sake, but Joey hesitantly lifted the needle off the disc.

Still carrying the food I made for him, I walked into each room, looking for the bearded man in robes. Joey's apartment was small, even more so than mine, and the doubt quickly formed in my mind as to having seen someone else at all. The amount of baggage and rubbish in here was piled to the ceiling in heaps of such disarray that looking in any direction created hints of monsters and madness peeking from under skewed cases. An assortment of footlockers rose above my head, stacked in ragged formation the way a brick wall appears after a cannonball has smashed through. Behind me, a pyramid of suitcases and cardboard boxes shifted like a wave. A mound of clothes spilled from an open closet, and a pungent smell leaked from its shadows.

And it was cold. Colder than the room should have been, colder than it *could* have been. Air conditioning was not a luxury afforded dependably at the Les Deux Oies. We sweated in our rooms most summer days, finding respite through box fans with damp clothes hung over them, listing strategically in each corner. But the fans did not blow today, and yet it was chilly as January's shore on Lake Erie.

I returned to the living room, and Joey still sat on the floor, knees pulled up to his gaunt chin.

"I told you he ain't here," Joey said.

"Do me a favor and don't listen to those records anymore," I said. Joey nodded, and his eyes looked in my direction, but they seemed to look *through* me, rather than at me. "I mean it, give it a break."

"Sure thing," he said. "I need a rest, anyway."

"I made you some eggs and soup. Where should I put it?"

"Anywhere, Charlie. I'm not that hungry."

"You need to eat. You look like you've lost thirty pounds over the week. In fact, you look like you need to go to the hospital."

If Joey had appeared wan and disheveled when I saw him in the hotel lobby on Tuesday, he was a soup sandwich now. His week's worth of whiskers were salt-and-pepper bristles turned splotchy as charred embers. His hair was dull and matted and hung over his ears. He still wore the same powder-blue button-down shirt from when I saw him last, and it looked now as if it could stand up on its own. But it was his skin that was the worst. It looked watery—translucent—like if I examined close enough I could see his bones and guts underneath. It's how I expected a man who was starving to death to look after a couple months, not just a few days.

"No hospital, Charlie. I just need some rest," he said. "I haven't been sleeping so well lately. The bearded man follows me in my dreams. He wants me to listen... he's trying to save me."

"The more you talk, the worse you sound."

He shook his head at an odd angle, the way someone does after swimming and trying to get water out of their ears. "Sorry, pal, I'm all right. Just this cold, you know? Makes me say funny things."

"Speaking of cold, it's freezing in here. How'd you get the superintendent to install working air conditioning?"

"Wetzel? He wouldn't do me any favors. He's been up here twice complaining the music's too loud."

"At least I'm not the only one who thinks those records are bad news."

"I don't know what it's all about, Charlie. I just have this compulsion—a *craving*—to keep listening. Even when I think I've turned it off, it's still playing."

I, too, felt the pull of the music, and how long had I listened to it total? Including when I walked in, maybe ten minutes, tops. How did Joey feel, who spent every day of last week locked in here alongside the gramophone and discs? I could only imagine the influence it held over him, an influence that seemed to become *stronger*, while he somehow grew sicker.

"Joey, I've never said this before. Nobody loves collecting cases like me, but this record player, this *thing*, maybe you need to get rid of it."

"Not yet. I'll take a rest, but I need to figure it out. It's like shootin' craps—you can't be sure, but just know your number's coming up soon. I feel like that, there's something big about to happen, and I don't want to miss it. I'm so close, Charlie... ready to make a great leap... I know it."

"Well, wait on it awhile. My friend, the Hungarian who runs a book store, told me to return this morning. He was going to research into what these records are saying."

Joey brightened at that. "I'd love to hear all about it."

"Why don't you come with me? Fresh air would do you good."

"No, like I said, I need to rest. That'll sort me out."

"Okay, sleep it off. I'll come back later and check on you. I mean it about maybe needing the hospital, though. You look bad."

"Thanks for the concern. I appreciate it, although you're starting to sound a bit like my mother." He grinned, and it looked almost as if his face split, the lines of his smile dissecting colorless cheeks like tearing across wet paper.

"And don't listen to those records," I added.

"Okay, Ma. Are you going to dress me and send me to Sunday School, too?"

I shook my head slow. "That's some sauce coming from a guy who says records are speaking to him."

Joey laughed at that, a great bellow that warmed the cold apartment. His head tilted back, and a hint of color returned to his milky eyes, and everything seemed as it should. The old Joey Third was back and in control. That's how I choose to remember him, laughing away the sickness, the dreams, the haunted records, laughing like he won the richest bag at the auction.

Though I saw Joey once more, I never heard him laugh again.

AMBASSADOR
BRIDGE
-SL-
©2020

5.

I RETURNED TO Vic's Books, driving parallel to the Detroit River most of the way. The blue-green water sparkled and lapped against the piers of Ambassador Bridge. It was a nice drive, which I should have found peaceful, but instead I traveled wrapped in melancholy thoughts. I arrived at the shop and entered as before, the small bell over the door announcing my presence. It was only a week since last I visited, but already the store seemed staler than before, mustier, as if the books were rotting dead things on the shelves of a crumbling mausoleum.

Strange, I thought, *how your surroundings are interpreted to reflect your mood.* When I entered last week, the store felt comfortable, reminding me of happy childhood memories, escaping from the world through imaginary portals created by the likes of Robert Louis Stevenson or H. Rider Haggard. Now the shop felt only dreary and old, a reminder of things that age and are shelved in obscurity.

I moved between the aisles of tomes and found Vic as before, sitting behind the counter and reading, a smoldering cigar stub planted between hardened lips.

"Charlie," he said, placing a marker between the pages of his book. "Right on schedule."

"If nothing else, I am a timely man." I spoke in full confidence but knew that if Gail were there, she'd laugh in my face.

"Timely *and* intriguing," Vic replied. He brought up the pillowcase of records and set them on the counter.

I was going to ask what he meant, but Vic just waggled an accusatory finger at my chest. He exhaled a ring of blue-gray fumes then stubbed out the cigar in a ceramic dish. "I got a friend to listen to your records. The language is Russian… mostly. My friend wants to know what kind of a gag this is, though."

I shook my head. "No gag, unless it was pulled off by whoever made the records."

"No backward words or dubbed-over voices?"

I shook my head again.

"Subliminal messages like that Elvis-kid plays in his music to make all the girls turn goo-goo for him?"

His questions began to irk me, as if this were a set-up and the real gag was being played on me. "Not that I know of, Vic. If I knew what the records were saying, I wouldn't have bothered you in the first place."

"My friend's name is Yefim László. He works with the Eastern Orthodox antiquities market. He says these are records of the dead."

"Records of the dead?" I repeated. "What does that mean?"

"There are sacred hymns that are chanted and, if performed correctly, lead one's soul to remain intact in another realm after the body fails. It's a sort of spiritual transcendence, or a method of immortality." Vic paused and steepled his fingers under his chin. "The interesting thing about this legend is that it dates back to the Indus Valley People of ancient Pakistan. You ever heard of them?"

"No… "

"They were a civilization of about twenty million people that vanished a few thousand years ago."

"How could twenty million people vanish?"

"That's the mystery, ain't it?"

I clenched my teeth. Vic could be infuriating sometimes.

He continued. "Of course, that was way before there were devices to record sound. You know the expression that photography is a means of immortality?"

"Sure, it's a way to be remembered forever."

"Consider what that statement means, because it ain't just for photographs. The idea holds true for any medium that records an image or a thought: paintings on cave walls, sculptures from stone, ink on papyrus. Those were *visual* recordings. Then Thomas Edison came along and invented the record player. The legend moved forward along with the advancement of technology. Voices and these hymns could be recorded, so their incantation—their essence—lasts forever."

Goosebumps prickled the flesh on my arms as I thought back, listening to the words spoken by people that were long-dead yet still hanging around. "Why did your friend think this was a gag?"

"He's from Moscow and has a passing familiarity with most of the Baltic languages. The dialect of Russian spoken on these records is old, but there are other languages, voices, he's never heard. Yefim described them as speech patterns like ancient Latin but spoken backward and guttural, as if recited through a mouth filled with mud."

Vic looked at me, reading for an expression. I didn't know what to say so forced out something, feeling obligated to reciprocate his remarks. "You don't say."

"Charlie," Vic said and leaned in close. "My friend says these records are cursed. They're like reading a demon's diary, they make you sick if you listen. They don't play like normal records. You noticed that already. And Yefim... he says they don't *end*."

I felt my guts sink to my knees. I thought back to when I listened to the albums, how they went on indefinitely, how I tired of listening and turned them off, though I never tried to listen all the way until it stopped. The air in Vic's store felt muggier, *thicker*, and I rubbed at the back of my neck, as if some presence breathed on me from behind. I was about to thank Vic for helping me out, make a quick exiting remark, and then get outside for some fresh air. But he continued.

"One more thing," he said.

"There's more?"

"You want me to quit now, or you want to hear the rest of what's on these records?"

"I'm still here, ain't I?"

"Not long ago there lived a Russian mystic who was said to have learned how to pass between the realms of the living and the dead. Maybe he did it through the hymns of the Indus Valley People or maybe not, but he believed that true salvation came from within, that the spirit of God lived in the heart, not in heaven above. The soul must be *conditioned* for the afterlife, or it would wither into nothingness like a flower, whose roots can't find perch in the soil.

"That man was Grigori Rasputin, the *Mad Monk*. These were his records."

I felt that presence on the back of my neck suddenly burn, like a bull's snort, and I needed to sit. My first thought was that I wanted Vic to keep the records, I didn't want to ever touch them again. But my next thought—the avarice within—wondered as to their value.

Vic seemed to read my mind. "I don't know of any self-respecting establishment that would want these in their possession." He ran his hand over the bundle. "Of course, this *is* Detroit, so not many places here respect themselves *that* much. I could probably put you in contact with a couple collectors of dark artifacts. Maybe get fifty bucks for each disc."

"Sure, thanks, Vic. Like I said before, these don't belong to me. I'm just doing a buddy a favor, asking on his behalf. But I know there ain't much he won't put a price tag on, so I'm sure he'll be interested."

"Yefim told me he doesn't ever want to see or hear these records again, and he was pretty insistent I stress that you should follow his sentiment. In other words, I'll cross his name off the list of possible buyers." Vic winked at his own joke.

"Thanks again."

"Nothing of it. Your thanks are reflected by your patronage." He extended his arms out to the bookshelves. "I'm sure you'll find something of interest."

I wasn't much in the reading mood, but I thought I could pick up a gift for Gail, maybe a fiction novel by Valerie Taylor or Faith Baldwin. Gail loved to bury herself in the risqué pulps late at night while we lay in bed. I started to turn away, to skim the shelves for her, when something clicked in my thoughts.

I needed to know more...

"Say, Vic, you got any books on Rasputin?"

-SL-
©2020

6.

I WANTED TO tell Joey what I found out and, like I promised, I said I'd return. So an hour later I stood back outside his apartment. It was quiet, and I silently thanked whatever angels were hanging around that he wasn't still playing those damned records. I knocked twice and tried the knob. The door was locked. I could have let myself in again, but I didn't want to seem like a nosy-Nelly, constantly checking on him, walking into his home whenever I felt like it. Anyway, I figured he was probably sleeping.

Another reason I decided to turn tail and get away quick was that I felt its pull again. The turntable was still spinning, still calling to me. It might not have been playing at that moment, but I knew it sure wasn't "off" either, in the sense of regular mechanical devices resting sedentary while not in use. A part of me began jonesing to hear it, a slobbering, sweating part that somehow slid Joey's key up into my hand and lifted it to the lock. I thought that must be how an addict feels, a fiend shootin' heroin into his arm every day who decides to go clean, until someone dangles a needle before his eyes.

A whisper snuck into my ears.

Ne zaderzhivat'sya v kholodnyy i temnyy, ho prisoyedinit'sya ko mne v svet navsegda.

I'm not ashamed to admit that I bolted, just turned and sprinted like Jessie Owns in Berlin. The whisper's allure didn't lessen until I rose in the elevator two floors above.

Back in my apartment I deadbolted the door, then paced between boxes, feeling my heart beat staccato. I went to the largest window and gazed outside for several minutes, letting the oceans of blue sky wash away the jitters. Most of the other tenants had views of identical apartments across the street: faded gray produce shops on the bottom level, stacked on top by floors of living quarters for the low-income populace of the city. Fortunately, my apartment's windows faced an empty lot, a barren space in the commercial quarters like the missing tooth from a child's mouth. I had as nice a view as I could hope for and, unobstructed, my place was kept well-lit. The early afternoon sun poured in, splashing the living room in soft hues the color of melted butter, and I began to feel better. I pushed aside a crate of cleaners and outdated calendars, set the pillowcase and records down on the kitchen table, and settled into my easy chair.

Though I wasn't in the reading mood, I looked at the book I'd bought from Vic. It was a biography of Rasputin, written by an ex-disciple who only distanced himself from Rasputin's teachings decades after the mystic's death. Quoted text proclaimed: *The shackles of my soul were loosed, the blinders removed...*

The front cover showed a photograph of Rasputin in middle-aged years, raising his hand in the air like the blade of a knife, while his mouth opened in a great void as if the camera caught him mid-sentence. His hair and beard were wild, like a billowing, unfolding creature. But it was his eyes that were most disconcerting. Those eyes were bulging wide, so large they looked as if a child had drawn a cartoon over his features. They were round orbs of snow-white, with specks of coal as the pupils, arched upward toward the heavens. It was a sinister image, and I wondered not at all how he gained his moniker, the *Mad Monk*.

I turned to the first page and began to read.

Grigori Yefimovich Rasputin is one of the strangest and most deviant men in modern history. He is remembered as a Russian holy monk and prophet with numerous proven incidences of healing that mystified the most educated medical minds of his time. He was also labeled a charlatan who manipulated the suffering of others for political and financial gain. Still today, he is regarded as a shadowy and furtive individual said to have been in league with supernatural forces and granted mystic abilities in exchange for dark servitude. The only fact which has been steadfastly proven is that Rasputin possessed some abnormal power over Russia's last ruling Emperor, Nicholas II and his family, and was instrumental in the fall of the tsarist government, which led to the collapse of the Romanov Dynasty in 1917.

Separating fact from superstition and heresy is challenging, as much written documentation relating to Rasputin has inexplicably been destroyed over the years since his death. Even that which I saw and experienced firsthand while under his sway seems difficult to believe and recite all these years later.

Rasputin was born a peasant sometime between 1863 and 1873 in a small village outside Siberia...

I read further. Soft tick-tocks from the clock on my wall punctuated each turned page. I was familiar with Rasputin's name as a mythical figure footnoted in school studies I'd once skimmed through as a boy but never read intimately. The mystic was said to have had two siblings, both of whom died young due in separate drowning-related incidents. And, unrelated to those mishaps, Rasputin himself also nearly drowned; it was only after his watery near-death that he began to portray indications of supernatural powers.

A court record found in the crumbling vault of Verkhoturye Monastery states that while Rasputin was aged "near-to-manhood," his father, Efim, had his horse stolen. It was claimed that Rasputin was able to envision the theft through a "sense known only to him," and lead armed men to a remote farm where the horse was found and the thief apprehended.

When eighteen, Rasputin was reportedly visited by the Virgin Mary and urged to join the Khlysty sect, an outlawed religious group that practiced exaltation through sexual ecstasy. He practiced his beliefs, "converting" the peasant women of each village he passed through. Indeed, his surname, "Rasputin," soon became synonymous in Russian as "the debauched one"...

An image worked itself into my mind of Rasputin as a conman, preying on the lonely borough wives whose husbands were gone while conscripted to labor or military service. Like hoods I knew in the shadows of Detroit, those granted the cunning and discipline to evade scruples found life to be a flea market, buying peoples' trust with words flimsy as a three-dollar bill. Religion and sex go hand-in-hand, after all, each just manners to escape the difficulties of everyday life, to find meaning in a troubled existence.

I read on, absorbing the details of his life, trying to understand the motivation behind stories of his exploits, his wanderings and dark lusts. I searched for a common theme stitching together his philosophies, failures, allies, and enemies; the cults he formed, the followers acquired through practices no other human could replicate.

Rasputin's rise to royal influence came about through his healing of Tsar Nicholas II's only son, young Aleksei, who was dying from hemophilia, a medical condition that impairs the body's ability to stop bleeding. From that time forward, Rasputin was deemed a "holy man" and a friend of the ruling family. His influence extended amongst the Tsar's wife, children, court nobles, and even bishops in the Orthodox Church.

With his political fortitude established, Rasputin began to preach openly and without fear of consequence, of reveling in immoral acts and even consorting with spirits. He was found guilty, though never sentenced, of raping a nun. He spoke with the dead, prophesized the future, and ordered followers to his bidding, which included kidnapping, assault, and even murder. His disciples came to be known as "The Misbegottens," and I shamefacedly admit to naming myself among their number.

During the onset of World War I, in particular, the whispers of Rasputin's dark servitude seemed true. I was alongside him in Rome on June 28, 1914 and heard him speak in tongues never before heard. Yet sailors in the middle of the Caspian Sea swore in court that Rasputin boarded their vessel that very day and flew away on wings of black, carrying off the third mate. On June 28, also, Archduke Franz Ferdinand of Austria was assassinated in Sarajevo. Witnesses testified Rasputin chanted strange words and stood next to the man who shot Ferdinand.

The outside world seemed to fall away while I was engrossed in the book, and I lost track of the time that passed. My imagination filled with Rasputin and the absurd accusations leveled against him. No matter how evil the man's motivations may have been, what was claimed he caused—and was capable of doing—was simply physically and scientifically impossible. I began to disregard the pages I read as mere tabloid fare, similar to the science fiction books I bought from Vic. Just because a book title states it is a biography based on fact does not mean it hasn't been embellished with fine words to attract sales.

I skipped a few chapters, skimming for anything I could relate to...

By 1915, Rasputin claimed to foresee his own impending death. He sought the methodology to remain living even after dying, and became obsessed with the variants of immortality and of finding the means for souls to travel between the worlds of death and of the living. He said: "My hour will soon come. I have no fear but know that the hour will be bitter for you. I will suffer a great martyrdom... and will inherit the kingdom."

During the last months of his life, Rasputin was rarely seen, yet those closest to him vanished without explanation. It was said that he collected souls to fulfill the great prophecy of a vanished people.

I skipped more pages, until some compulsion caused me to flip halfway through and begin reading in earnest.

... When encountered at night, Rasputin was said to chant incessantly. He collected certain "words" according to their etymology, and he filled them with dark power, the way other men might fill a bucket with water. Such words that he spoke had much more meaning than their surface definition. Words that Rasputin empowered could become an invitation or a password, a remark shared like a secret handshake that, the more spoken, grew only in potency.

Words like, 'Vkhodite.'

My mouth unhinged, and every piece of baggage in my apartment seemed to gasp alongside me.

For Rasputin, 'vkhodite' was the ultimate communiqué of influence. Translating to "come in," the word became the banner command of submission and the proved intention to submit to his discipline. Vkhodite meant to "come into" his world, his dogma. You were surrendering yourself to a higher power, leaving behind the cold and fleeting solitude of earthly existence for immortality under his command. In effect, he was setting himself up as a god and his 'Misbegottens' as his disciples.

Rasputin would induct his followers as such: "Ne zaderzhivat'sya v kholodnyy i temnyy, ho prisoyedinit'sya ko mne v svet navsegda."

"Do not linger in the cold and dark, but join me in the light forever."

My God, it was the phrase from the music! Vic's friend *was* right; it really was Rasputin's records.

But if what this author—this former disciple—said was true, how did the chanting on the records hold such an influence over me and over Joey, who was becoming quite obsessed, just by listening to them now, years later? Did those words really hold such power?

I knew then that regardless of how much of the book was unembellished, I had to find a way to convince Joey to get rid of the records. The hoodoo-voodoo they spouted carried *some* sort of psychological consequence. I thought about calling Joey and laying it all out, but how could I convince him the few bucks he might turn on those records was worth the effect of a brainwash? I decided I'd go down there tomorrow, take him to breakfast, and lay it all out.

The phone rang, a shrill blast that caused me to leap from the chair like a frightened child. Though it startled me, it was nonetheless a welcome interruption from my dreary thoughts.

I caught my breath and answered. "Hello?"

"Hi." It was Gail, and I relaxed. She was a needed respite from what I'd just read. She continued. "What're you doing today?"

"Just thinking about you," I lied.

"Good answer."

"Yourself?"

"Home from work early and wondering if you'd like to come over for a Friday night date. I'm going to make chicken and artichoke, and there's a bottle of chardonnay that takes two to drink."

I needed to break and take some time to contemplate

matters. An evening at Gail's seemed like a shipshape idea. "Sure, honey. Any special occasion?"

"Well... " her voice softened. "I want to talk. You know, about us."

Oh God, I thought. '*The Talk*.' What I first thought as a 'shipshape idea' now sank like the *Titanic*. Call me misogynistic, but when a woman makes plans just to talk, it means she probably wants something that requires an unfavorable change of your lifestyle.

I gritted my teeth, but tried to keep my voice upbeat. "I'd like that. What time were you thinking?"

"I know how busy you are," she said. My anxiety slipped into defensiveness, as if that were a barb against me for not having a real job. Just thinking about *The Talk* flipped my emotions topsy-turvy. She continued. "What's a good time for you?"

"I can make time whenever you like," I replied.

"I mean, what time can you commit to? Punctuality isn't one of your finer points, and I don't want dinner going cold."

Another barb? I already wished I had said I was too busy to meet. "How about at five? That's two hours from now. I'll start getting ready and maybe even arrive early to show what a changed guy I can be."

"Just on-time is good enough. I can't wait to see you," she said.

"You too. I'm really looking forward to it."

A knock sounded at the front door.

"Someone's at the door," I said. "Gotta go, but I'll see you later."

"Okay, five o'clock. Love you."

"Love you too."

I hung up the phone, first feeling grateful for the interruption, then feeling guilty for feeling grateful. I went to the door.

It was Ray, bearing a big smile and a clipboard.

"Hey, Charlie, how's it going?"

"Just living life. What brings you by?"

"We had a hot date, remember? Three o'clock, I'm here to peruse the knickknacks you've been hoarding."

Nuts. I knew I was destined to be late to Gail's. Again.

"Actually, slipped my mind," I said. "I'm not really prepared—"

"Sounds like you need a secretary." He pushed his way inside and whistled. "And a housekeeper."

I had to imagine what my apartment looked like to someone for the first time. Although I knew Ray expected it—the only difference between us being that he owned stores to place his auction winnings into instead of piling them in his living room—I still felt the scarlet blushes of shame. The walls of luggage I collected looked like the hedges at City Park, cut into an elaborate maze where one could wander lost all day. I don't know how I let it build up so much; it was overwhelming to think of the day I'd ever have to clear it all out.

Inspiration struck. I said, "I'll cut you a deal if you take away everything all at once."

Ray just rolled his eyes. "Funny. Most of this you couldn't give to the homeless."

"So you came all the way over here to insult me?"

He snapped his fingers and slapped my back. "Don't get so tense. I know there's valuables in here I can pay cash for."

"All right. You want to start over there?" I said. I led him to a half-wall separating my dining area from the kitchenette.

I'd created impromptu shelving out of luggage stacked in different directions and, in the spaces created, stored a deluge of kitschy sculptures, glassware, and tin devices whose purposes were meaningless to me. "I've got some curiosities that came from an Egyptian bagman."

"Egyptian is always a good start."

After half an hour, Ray had ferreted through only a corner of my collections. I started getting antsy, watching the time. I originally thought he might only take a cursory glance, buy a few things, and be off, but he buried himself inside mountains of suitcases that I hadn't looked at in years. He reminded me of an archaeologist, carving through the substrate with a hand spoon, carefully logging every detail in a grid of sectioned quadrants. I wanted to tell him to speed it up, but he was so thorough, setting aside things I forgot—or maybe never knew—I possessed, including jade teacups from China, Mediterranean lithographs, a Royal Air Force jacket, and Art Deco-era dining utensils made of colored glass. Money signs danced before my eyes.

"I gotta make a call," I said.

"It's your place."

I dialed Gail, hoping she hadn't gotten too started on dinner, and fumbled through my mind a number of excuses as to why I would be late. The phone just rang. I let it jangle twenty times, then hung up and called again. Still no answer. I cursed three shades of blue. Tonight wouldn't go well if she had a big talk planned and I blew it off.

I considered Ray a good friend, but not good enough to leave in my home unattended where he could "find" something and take it away without telling me—I simply would never know if anything went missing. But his bright excitement caught me; every few minutes he was muttering *wow* under his breath and setting things aside, and I knew I was earning money just watching him.

On the other hand, no amount of money was worth the guilt of skipping on Gail's dinner.

"Ray," I said. "I hate to interrupt you, but I'm going to have to ask you to wrap it up."

"You kicking me out already, Charlie? I thought we were doing business."

"We are, but we'll have to pick up another time. I'm sorry. It's my fault I overbooked today."

"I came all the way across the city for this."

"Don't chafe. I think you could spend all week in here and still not be done."

"If you let me." His eyes twinkled. "You've got some notable effects stashed in your belongings."

The phone rang, and I prayed it was Gail checking on me, knowing I was running late. Maybe I could salvage this afternoon after all.

"Hold that thought," I told Ray. Into the phone, I answered, "Hello?"

"Charlie, I've got an offer for you."

It was Vic. Normally I'd be happy to hear from him, but now wasn't a good time. Then again, anytime was good to hear an offer.

"I'm listening," I said.

"My friend, Yefim László—the one who listened to your records—wants to buy them."

"I thought he never wanted to see or hear them again."

"That's what he told me, but I guess people are allowed to change their minds. He's here now, and he wants them."

"They're not my records to sell—they're my friend, Joey's, downstairs. I'll have to arrange a meeting between them for another time."

"Yefim is hot to buy right now."

"It'll have to wait. I'm in the middle of a couple other deals."

Vic's voice lowered, as if he were whispering. "Charlie, I've never seen my friend like this. I tried talking him out of it, but he's prepared to spend a great deal of money to procure those records immediately. He says time is of the essence. Maybe he learned something we don't know, but your friend could be in for a windfall."

My nerves burned. I was about to tell Vic there wasn't a chance in Hades I would set up a meeting right now with Joey as sick as he was and me running so late. But then I thought, *this was an out*. Those records were no good—I knew that in a way that didn't make logical sense—and maybe this was a way to get rid of them. Whoever's hands they ended up in would be away from Les Deux Oies. Somebody else could figure out those hellish chants and dreams of a crazy man.

I hoped Gail would understand... she'd have to.

I spoke into the phone. "I can't guarantee Yefim an audience with my friend, as he's been real sick lately. But he can come over and I'll bring him down for an introduction."

I heard Vic relay my response to Yefim and then his excited reply.

"I'm in the Les Deux Oies building," I said. "On Sanford Street. Sixth floor, apartment number six-twelve."

"Yefim gives his thanks and is on his way."

"All right. Thanks, Vic."

"And, Charlie," he said. "Don't fleece him too badly. I've never seen Yefim like this, so... desperate."

We hung up, and I saw Ray standing nearby, acting inconspicuous, but obviously listening to the whole conversation.

"What was that all about?" he asked innocently.

"People are going to think we're holding a convention in here. Another collector's coming over."

"And this after you tell me I have to leave?"

"I'm bringing him down to Joey's place. He wants to buy some records Joey won last week."

"What kind of records?"

"The kind you don't want," I said.

Ray snapped his fingers once, loud. His face tightened into a scowl. "Charlie, I hope you're not holding out on me. Who buys your wins when nobody else does? I throw myself at you, offering you dough. And here you are giving the inside scoop to another dealer? I think I should get the right to bid, too."

"Ray," I said and paused, not knowing how to explain myself without sounding four cents shy of a nickel. "The records are no good, trust me. They're in another language, and they hurt your ears, they sound so bad."

"Yet someone wants to buy them this very moment."

"I don't know what this guy wants them for, but it's a bad investment."

"Maybe I can judge for myself."

My exasperation was growing out of control. I felt people were walking all over me with what they wanted, and I couldn't put my foot down hard enough to control them. "Fine, but I'm telling you it's a waste of your time."

Ray nodded slightly. "We'll see," he said, and went back to rifling through the suitcases.

I tried calling Gail again, but she still didn't answer. I wondered if it was on purpose—she knew that if she picked up, I'd snake my way into canceling, but if I couldn't get a hold of her, the guilt would drive me to rush over there one way or the other. Which was true. I heard that rich socialites were beginning to use "answering machines," like robotic secretaries, and that someday it would be commonplace for every phone to automatically have the ability to record a message. Did I wish we used that technology today...

I didn't have time remaining to shower and shave like I wanted, but I got cleaned up as best I could in the shortened amount of time. I planned to drop off Yefim and Ray at Joey's and go from there straight to Gail's. I towel-washed my face in the sink, trying not to look too hard at the features of my weathered mug. Gail said the wrinkles around my mouth and the crow's feet at my eyes gave me "movie star character," but I thought they just made me look prematurely old. Not that I cared much about my appearance. I had never been a lady's man in the looks department and, as I aged, I knew it mattered less and less.

I wound my way through stacks of baggage until I reached the closet. I pushed aside uniforms, and costumes, and vintage finery until I reached my own clothes, and selected a charcoal gray suit with olive pinstripes. I heard a tumbling thud from the living room, followed by a clattering like loose coins rolling across a tile floor.

"I'm all right," Ray called from the living room. "Some of your cases took a tumble."

I didn't reply. Just dug around until I found some clean dress socks and shoes that weren't dull enough to need a shine. Picked out a silk tie that was soft as clouds. It was one of six dozen found inside a lacquered salesman's trunk I won at an auction last year. That had been a good bid; I'd never have to buy a tie again for the rest of my life.

I knotted it, and someone pounded at the front door. Pushing my way past luggage towers, I returned to the living room, where Ray scoffed. I answered the door, prepared to feel the embarrassment of someone else seeing my place for the first time. The man who answered was old and wiry with the biggest shock of white hair I'd ever seen, overlaying his head like an enormous cotton ball. He was pale, and shook slightly, and barely looked around.

"Mr. Charlie Stewart?" he asked.

"That's me. You must be Yefim."

"Yes. I'm very excited to hear those records again."

"Come in," I said. I motioned at Ray. "That's Ray. Ray, Yefim."

Ray was suddenly all smiles. He snapped his fingers and plunged his hand into Yefim's. "Nice to meet you," he said.

Yefim returned the handshake but barely acknowledged him.

"You listened to the music, yes?" Yefim asked me.

I nodded. "I heard it."

"Has *he* come to you? The man with the beard?"

My chest tightened, as if a vice wrapped around my ribs and pressed in.

"Who's that?" Ray asked. "Another dealer?"

I flashed him the 'not now' look.

"Yeah, I think I've glimpsed a bearded man. What does it mean?" I asked.

"Hasn't he told you?" Yefim answered. "Or are you not listening?"

"That doesn't exactly answer my question."

"It means there's room for all of us."

My chest tightened more, if that were possible. I thought of the dreams of people grouped around a campfire in the snow. "You've got it worse than Joey."

"He can save you also, if you let him."

"Who are you talking about?" My voice rose. "Who is the man with the beard?"

Yefim's voice was proper, crisp. "It is Rasputin. But I think you knew that already. He's returned as prophesized."

The vice, tighter. There was barely room in my chest to inhale.

"The world is ending soon, Mr. Stewart. Rasputin is here to save us, if you accept him."

"Wow," Ray said and snapped his fingers. "Rasputin?"

Yefim nodded gravely.

"You've got records by the Russian seer, Rasputin?"

"Mr. Stewart's friend has them. He is *the doorway*."

Ray smiled for all the wrong reasons. "Then what are we doing up here?"

Staying safe, I wanted to respond. But I knew I had to move; it was time to go to Joey's.

"What are you going to do with the records?" I asked Yefim.

"The same as anyone would do. Listen to them."

Suddenly my plan seemed foolish, the strategy of a child who breaks a cookie jar and tries to hide it in the nearest cupboard drawer. I would never be able to contain this mess just by passing it along for someone else to use.

"I hear it playing now," Yefim added. "Below us... "

I thought of the three records that Vic passed to Yefim. Vic had said: *"My friend says these records are cursed. They're like reading a demon's diary; they make you sick if you listen. They don't play like normal records. You noticed that already. And Yefim... he says they don't end."*

I wondered how long Yefim had listened to those records while they were in his possession. Did he play them for hours before realizing they never ended? Was he more *infected* with it than any of us? The music seemed like a germ. Once it contaminated you, you might not feel its effects for some time... but then the germ incubates, it infects the listener and spreads into madness. Yefim must have understood after listening that they were cursed and returned them to Vic, but since then the voices grew in his head, calling to him to listen again.

"Below us... " Yefim repeated. He cocked his head, listening to a song I could not hear. He walked out the door.

What could I do? Stop him by force? The records would still play, and Joey would still listen. I decided my original child's strategy would have to do for now. If Yefim took them, at least that would buy me some time. At least the records would be out of the building and, hopefully, their effect diminished on us here.

I followed Yefim down the hall to the elevator, and Ray trailed after us, writing in his clipboard.

"I'll help you get the records," I told Yefim. "But you take them far, far away from here."

He didn't respond, and the elevator doors opened to take us inside.

I heard that cursed music as soon as we reached Joey's floor. I imagined a rider on a horse galloping to me from the distance. Every time I heard the records playing, the rider drew closer and closer, great puffs of dust filling the sky behind. Only that rider wasn't coming to greet me—he was coming to run me down.

Yefim seemed almost to be shaking, like he was overjoyed to hear the sound. Ray made a face like someone farted in his ear and told him it was a lullaby.

I had sensed those records were bad news ever since I first listened to them, but now I began to feel genuinely scared. It was harder each time I heard it not to just settle down and let it carry me off to whatever dream world it sang about. I fought the temptation and led the others to Joey's door, thinking, *let Yefim take the records away; please just let him take them all right now.* That was followed by the thought that if Yefim didn't buy every one of the records, I would snatch them with me on the way out. Just grab-and-dash, break them over my knee, and apologize later.

We walked down the hall, and I saw the building's superintendent, Horace Wetzel, standing in a daze outside Joey's apartment. His craggy face hung slack and tilted toward the door as if listening to what occurred on the other side.

"Wetzel, what're you doing?" I asked.

He looked at me confused, the expression of someone waking from a deep slumber.

"I got a complaint," he said. "A complaint... but someone called me... someone I couldn't see... "

"So you settled for eavesdropping?"

His mind seemed to clear a bit, and his face flushed. "I run this building. I can go where I damn well please."

"I don't think nosing around is in your job description—"

"You got a problem, pay your rent on time. Then we'll talk," he interrupted.

He turned about-face and marched up the hall toward the elevators. His head kept twitching to the side, though, as he passed, spasms like the aftershock of a violent sneeze.

I knocked at Joey's door, knowing he wouldn't answer. I turned the knob and the door opened, so I entered, followed by Yefim and Ray.

The first thing I saw was that Joey wasn't alone. There were several other men and women sitting with him in a circle on the floor. The Scandinavian, Martin, sat hunched over, arms extended palms-up, as if offering worship to Joey. Next to him, Martin's wife tilted her face to the ceiling, eyes rolled back. The woman across the hall with blue hair was there, swaying back-and-forth, as were a couple other people who looked familiar, but I didn't know by name.

The man with the beard was there, too... *Rasputin*. This time he did not vanish when I looked upon him.

He stood behind Joey, and a strange effect caused me to rub at my eyes. The room seemed blurry, as if a fine mist hung in the air. I looked again and saw Rasputin was also *within* Joey, like a spirit rising from its mortal body or, perhaps, like a form within a form, like those little Russian nesting dolls, in which a wooden figure is stacked inside another wooden figure.

The chanting was louder than ever before. The record player must have been at full volume and everyone in the room sang with it. That sound was hideous: squealing, crashing, scratching instruments that just played over and over, overlaid by the recorded voices. Yefim pushed past me to kneel with the others and began to repeat the words I now knew so well.

Vkhodite. Vkhodite. Vkhodite.

Ne zaderzhivat'sya v kholodnyy i temnyy, ho prisoyedinit'sya ko mne v svet navsegda.

"Christ almighty, it's cold in here," Ray said softly. Then he gasped. "Is that... snow?"

And then I realized why the room seemed blurry. There was a fine veil of snowflakes floating in the air. The baggage stacked against the walls had thin lines of frost hanging off the edges. On top of the nearest stack lay the empty leather suitcase with ivory handle that Joey had won, the case that had contained the record player. Everything in the room seemed paler than it should have been.

Yefim turned to us. "Come in," he said. A puff of fog exhaled with his breath. "Do not linger in the cold."

He returned to chanting, and I felt shammed. Yefim was never planning on buying the records; he just feigned interest in order to find out where they were. He wanted to hear them again, to join with the others.

"Charlie," Ray said and tugged at my elbow. "What's going on?"

"It's those records."

I looked again at Joey and stepped closer to him. I was wrong in thinking Rasputin was "within" him. It was the other way around; Joey was within Rasputin and fading away. I saw Joey only as if he were an afterimage. Rasputin's eyes glowed like burning coal briquettes, and they shone through the veil of snow. Steam lifted off his shoulders. If we were in a snowy forest, it was Rasputin who would be the campfire that we circled for warmth.

"Joey," I said. "Can you hear me?"

The group chanted louder.

I needed to turn the music off, to set them free. I pushed past Joey's neighbors and reached for the gramophone playing in their midst. Rasputin watched me and made no effort to interfere. I should have been leery when a thin smile crossed his face, but I moved forward in my charge with the adrenaline-fueled fortitude of the sanctimonious.

I took hold of the record player's arm and lifted. It took no more than a second, and it was *easy*. The music stopped and, by proxy, so did the chanters. It was as if the spell were broken immediately, and the room turned dead-silent. I was already imagining squeezing my hands around that bearded lunatic's throat.

Of course there had to be a reason he was known as the 'Mad Monk'; I should have realized he kept some sort of hoodoo up his sleeves in order to skip across time and materialize out of a record player.

The player's brass arm turned fluid in my fingers and moved like a wet snake, lashing out with its needle, slicing the palm of my hand. A bright red line opened across my skin, and I released it with a cry. The arm became solid again and dropped back exactly into the position from where I had lifted it. The music—and the chanting—resumed.

Rasputin now spoke, and licks of flame shot from his mouth. "Come in. Do not linger in the cold."

An icy wind blew over me, and Rasputin's robes billowed with a *poof*. I felt light-headed listening as the chanting continued, but it sounded distant, the volume turned down. The air became fuzzier, and I wrapped my arms across my chest, shivering under the thin pinstriped suit.

Why had I come into the snow dressed like this?

Pine trees bristled thick in all directions, and I knew I would be lost if I tried to make my way amongst them by myself. In the distance, on mountaintops, were fairy-tale castles with pink and turquoise spires. The moonlight caused them to glow. Snowflakes settled on my nose, and I felt myself grow numb. It was an effort of great magnitude to lift my legs and move, though there was nowhere I could go. I stood in a clearing with a campfire at its center. The fire was wrapped in robes and a beard.

Vkhodite.

Rasputin rose into the air and held up his hands parallel to each other, about a foot apart, as if supporting an invisible rod at each end. Between his hands, the universe shifted. I saw flames roll across the cosmos, obliterating worlds and stars and gods. The infinitesimality of existence consumed my thoughts, much as the flames consumed eternity. I knew not if this were a reflection of the past, or of things to come, or how I fit in, only that I was as insubstantial in its effect as a shadow is in a lightless cave. If I held poison in my hand, I would have drunk it; had I a gun, I would have put it to my head. The despair was a blanket wrapped over my senses, so that I suffocated in its many folds.

Vkhodite.

Then I knew. He showed me these things so I would join him. He offered an escape, a freedom from suffering, a chance to find new purpose as one of his Misbegottens. I would never again be alone, never shiver in the snow of life. *I would never die.* It was only my soul he would take, a pittance for his gift of immortality, and I would play on and on through him. If only I would stop fighting and chant along to the music...

I woke to Ray slapping my face. He wore a silver pinky ring in the shape of a horseshoe, and the edge of its band cut my cheek.

"Snap out of it," he said and shook me like a ragdoll.

The temperature seemed to jump a hundred degrees. I went from standing in drifts of snow to leaning against Ray in the muggy early evening of Detroit summer.

"I gotta slap you again?" he asked.

Ray seemed blurry at first but soon drifted into focus. I spoke, and heard my voice sounded drugged. "No."

"Thought you went loopy on me."

"What happened?"

Ray let go of me. We stood on the sidewalk outside Les Deux Oies.

"You were talking to someone," he said. "And then your voice just dropped off. You looked like you were sleepwalking, the way you moved, real sluggish and stiff. You sat on the floor with your friends and mumbled some weird words over and over."

"Didn't you feel it?" I asked.

"Yeah, I felt it. That's why I left. I've been drunk enough to know when my senses are slipping away. I picked you up and carried you out."

"They didn't stop you?"

"The man with the beard said something, and the others looked like they might intervene, but you and I were close to the door. I was quick and, once out, nobody followed."

"Joey needs help," I said.

"He sure does. I don't know what he's gotten himself into. What were they doing up there? Looked like a group of commies praying to the devil. That's some sick stuff." Ray snapped his fingers.

"We've got to stop them."

"You have a plan? I hope it don't involve the police, 'cause they wouldn't care. As long as it stays in the room, that's a solid case of religious freedom. Maybe McCarthy was right all along. We're being subverted by the *pinkos*. Ever since his censure, the liberals have been running the country."

Vkhodite.

It sounded in my head, from far away, calling to me. Was the voice growing stronger the longer it went on? Or did its reach expand as more people sang along?

"But you saw it," I said. "It's like being brainwashed. And for God's sake, it was snowing in there! Police or not, we have to go back, pull Joey out of the room, the same as you pulled me out. Then the others… "

"I don't think you're in a condition to do much of anything. You look like you died and thawed out."

I felt it too. The hot evening air burned my cold skin. My joints ached, and my brain felt like Willie Mays used it for batting practice. But I persisted. "He's my friend. I just… wasn't prepared."

"And you're still not. You're not thinking. What're you going to do differently the next time you go up there?"

I couldn't think of a thing.

Ray continued. "How long has Joey been up there with those records?"

"He's been gettin' an earful every day for the past week, trying to figure them out."

"So a little while longer's not going to change anything. We've got to take matters into our own hands, Charlie. We need weapons."

"You've got a gun?"

"I was at Normandy. I've got a collection."

"I didn't know you were in the army."

"Came back a goddamned war hero. Lot of good it does you after the headlines change."

I was taken aback—the things you don't know about your friends.

"So, what's your plan?" I asked.

Ray started snapping fast. "Like I said, we need weapons. I have to go to my North Side shop, I've got some things in storage there. Plus it'll help to have another man, and John's working all night, taking inventory. I'll bring him back armed for bear."

I was going to ask, "Which John," but I supposed it didn't matter.

"We'll regroup in the lobby," Ray said. "I would bring you along, but I've only got a two-seater, and John doesn't have a car. I think you need to rest up anyway."

I was torn inside. I couldn't let Joey rot away in his room any longer with that... *thing*. I wanted to get him now, but I felt faint, like I could topple over any moment and not get back up. Then again, was I lying to myself? Did I really want to go back up there to try to save Joey, or was I making up a reason to hear the music again, to let myself give up? I already felt lulled into a state of semi-hypnosis. The mind plays funny tricks sometimes, and I couldn't trust my own reasoning.

"All right," I conceded.

"You want me to help you back up to your room?" he asked.

"No, I need to get away, put some distance between myself and this building for awhile."

"Don't go far."

"I've just got somewhere I have to check in at."

Ray nodded. "We'll do it, Charlie, don't you worry. We'll storm them, just like at Normandy."

"What time?" I asked.

"What time is what?"

"What time should we meet back in the lobby?"

He stared at me, and his head twitched just barely. "Yeah, in the lobby. Um, three hours. Meet you here in the lobby... three hours, at ten o'clock."

I felt a brush of déjà vu, like I was experiencing something again, something that had occurred already. The air seemed a little colder, a little darker. Or possibly it was just the sun beginning to fall.

"Maybe I should follow you," I said, and I knew it was my fear working me over; I didn't want to be alone. I didn't have many lifelines to grasp, and he was the nearest. If something happened to Ray, my odds of beating this situation would slip even worse. "It could be better if we stay together. I'll just drive separate."

"Do you hear that?" he asked.

"Hear what?"

Ray looked at me and blinked. "No, I gotta go. Can't keep watching in the rearview for you. We'll meet back in the lobby."

I noticed he stopped snapping.

"In Normandy," he said. "Normandy... "

"Ray—"

"See you, Charlie." He turned about-face and left.

I found myself alone on the sidewalk. The streetlamp across the street turned on, then fizzled and went out. I walked the other way, around to the side of the building where tenants parked, still feeling muddled in the mind. The longer I was in the shadow of the apartments, I realized the honest truth was that I *did* want to go back to Joey's room and surrender to the song. I thought of my vision in Rasputin's world and the difficulty of moving each leg; that was how I felt now, as if I struggled to reach my car through a bank of snow. But if the others in Joey's room had given in, it was only because they hadn't been there from the beginning. They didn't see what it did to us, the way I watched Joey fade away. Maybe they believed this was a grand venture, a chance to discover the meaning of existence, but I didn't buy it. It was the devil's deal and a kick in the ass.

I made it to my car. I opened the door and slid behind the steering wheel. Slipped the key into the ignition and... nothing. The engine gurgled and belched but wouldn't roll over. I turned the key again to the same effect. I knew my transmission had been going out, but this was something different. The starter? Carburetor? Rasputin's effort? All I knew was the Crestline wasn't going anywhere tonight. How the world seems to conspire when desperation nips at your heels...

Vkhodite.

I needed to get away. I sensed Rasputin—that thing—reaching down to me from the fourth floor, his arms extending like wisps of flame. I jumped out of the car and ran back around the building, hoping to see Ray before he drove off. He was nowhere in sight, so I just kept on running, all the way down Sanford Street, past its closed shops and darkened windows and old vagabonds sleeping in the alleyways.

A taxi drove slowly in the other direction eyeing me: a middle-aged man running—now holding the stitch in his side and gasping for breath—down the street, dressed in a flapping suit and shoes in which one sole began to crack off. I waved him over and, fortunately, he didn't think I was too crazed. I gave him directions, and he drove me to Gail's.

It was after eight o'clock by the time I knocked on her front door. Gail's bungalow was an architectural turn-of-the-century wonder, cramming five split-level rooms and a kitchenette into only a thousand square feet of space. It might have been small, but Gail's home was sharp. Each room had its own theme and color palette; she decorated to match with the season's fashions. She even let me keep a room so I'd feel more welcome during visits. Of course, it never felt like "my" room without luggage littering under every step.

Knocking at her door reminded me of Joey; I rapped for half a minute without any response. I had a key to her house the same as I did for him, but didn't want to let myself inside if she was fuming.

Finally, she answered. I tried not to look too hard at the streaks of mascara dried under her eyes.

"I'm sorry I'm so late," I said. "I'm in some kind of mess."

Her eyes went big and pink lips parted like a blooming rose. "Charlie, what's wrong with you?"

"It's a long story, dear. It's Joey, I don't know what to do."

"No, it's you," she said. "You look sick. You're paler than a ghost."

"I am?"

"Lord, I can almost see through your skin."

The tension of the last several hours caught up to me, and I felt faint, like I would collapse right on her doorstep.

"Come in," she said. "You need to lie down."

She led me to the living room couch, and I sank down so quick, I thought I would fall through the floor.

"I'll get you some water," she said and vanished into the kitchenette.

When I woke, another hour had passed. Gail wrapped a couple blankets over me while I slept.

"You're freezing," she said.

"I'll be all right."

"I just called Dr. Adams, but he's out on another call. A nurse said to bring you into the hospital."

"It's only the snow," I said. "The snow's making me cold."

"What snow?"

I blanched... why had I said that? The snow was a dream...

Vkhodite.

It was a record, playing over and over again. That's why it kept repeating, like an album that got scratched; it played the same phrases in a loop, repeating through the disc's groove without moving forward. That's where I was, trapped inside the record's cycle.

I had to turn it off.

Gail stroked my forehead. The warmth of her touch thawed my chill. "Charlie, you're scaring me. What's going on?"

Was I drifting away again?

I bolstered myself to focus. "I—I'm hearing things... seeing things... that are real."

That didn't make any sense at all. She cocked her head and made a face, waiting for more. I finally spat it out, blunt as a brick. "Do you believe in ghosts?"

"Ghosts?" she repeated, and her eyes narrowed as if she were contemplating some underlying meaning to the question. "You mean like spirits that haunt our homes?"

Gail and I had spoken late into the night on many subjects, but the topics of death and religion were not ones we broached in-depth. I knew she affirmed Protestant leanings, as myself, but hadn't visited a church in decades. Perhaps religion, like death, was for the morbid.

"Yes, a presence after death," I replied.

"I think we have a soul, some sort of residue that transcends elsewhere, but I don't really believe in invisible people that remain, wandering amongst us."

"Gail," I said, and paused before continuing. "There's a ghost in Les Deux Oies. It's hurting people, and I think it's taking them away to another place. It's touched me... it's *inside* me somehow, and it's trying to take me, too."

I thought she would step back and roll her eyes and say how the hoarding in my apartment is truly driving me bonkers. Instead, she kept stroking my forehead and kissed my brow as her fingers passed over.

"What can I do to help?" she asked.

"You believe me?"

"If there's something affecting you, I'll do whatever it takes to make it right."

I don't know why, but I always seemed to judge myself more harshly than Gail judged me. My own conscience constantly thought the worst of myself, and it manifested itself onto her. She was the understanding one between us, the rational and considerate partner in our relationship. Even when I was late to see her or pulled a boneheaded move, I knew she would be inwardly disappointed, but she never made as big a deal of it as I did in my own mind. I got into the habit of thinking ill of people—even her—and then, every time when I braced myself for negativity, she amazed me with sympathy and understanding.

"I—I don't know what to do," I said.

"Tell me what happened."

And so I did. I recited everything from that previous Thursday night at the baggage auction where Joey won the record player. I described the chanting we heard and my conversations with Vic, trying to figure out what the music meant. I told her how I watched Joey grow wan, until I saw him last as nothing more than a shadow within Rasputin. I explained the music's effect on anyone who heard it, even Joey's neighbors who were hapless enough to be within earshot of his room. I spoke of the dreams I had and the impossible changes in his room, as if it transformed into another land.

I told Gail everything and, again, braced myself for her rebuke.

"Why on God's green earth are you still living there, if you think a curse is taking over the building?" she asked. "Just leave."

That wasn't the response I expected, though it seemed an obvious question to be asked.

"I believe it's like an infection," I said after careful thought. "It's a seed planted in my brain, and it won't be dislodged regardless of how far away I travel. I've been fighting it, but he's in my dreams, he's in my head, *whispering*. I've got to turn it off, forever."

Gail made a face like she was going to cry, then it seemed to change to a laugh, before returning to the potential waterworks. "Oh, God, the messes you get into, Charlie."

"This is hardly something you can plan on—"

She interrupted, as if I hadn't spoken. "If only I'd talked to you a couple weeks ago."

I didn't like the sound of that remark... a phrase like that could lead to a whole slew of problematic scenarios.

I asked anyway. "About what?"

"You seem so distracted when we're together, like your mind is somewhere else."

I knew better than to disagree with that.

She continued. "I didn't want to bring it up if it wasn't going to happen, but now it has, and I wish I'd have discussed it with you since the very beginning."

"What, Gail? I'm feeling crazy enough without you dragging up something else."

"Geoff Van Duyn made me a job offer to oversee onsite expansion of a new Rockwell's. I'm moving to New York City."

I was devastated. No, I was *crushed*. All the building fear and distress was a weight so great, it felt as if I crawled on concrete while a giant foot squashed me from above. And now here I sat, literally *dying*, and my girlfriend says she's leaving me. Though I'd always expected it, I wasn't prepared for that stab of pain that suddenly made all the other pain seem as inconsequential as a scratch on the thumbnail.

"I'm sorry," I said, more to myself than to her.

"I want you to come with me," she said.

"Huh?"

"Charlie, I know how happy you are in Detroit. You've got your friends, your collections. But what's your future here? You're struggling with something every time I see you. My relocation will be paid for and I'll be making good money, more than I need. It's a chance to start over for both of us... together."

My mind reeled, and I couldn't determine if it was Rasputin's curse knocking me or what Gail just said. "That's so... sudden."

"I know, Charlie. But sometimes when your train comes to station, you've got to be ready on the platform, suitcase in hand."

"Is that why you brought me to dinner with Van Duyn?"

"I wanted you to meet him. The promotion was a possibility, something rumored about that I was in the running for. He made me the offer today. I was planning on telling you over dinner tonight... under better circumstances."

"Congratulations." I wasn't sure of what else to say.

"I should have told you what it entailed earlier," she said. "But it was just a rumor, and I didn't want to get our hopes up, or make it seem like I was some girl suckered by daydreams."

"Gail, your timing—"

"Like I said, I wish I would have discussed this a couple weeks ago, when I first heard about it. Maybe you would have been packing your clothes instead of running around at those auctions. Maybe this *thing* never would have happened."

Though I appreciated her stance, I doubted I would have skipped on an auction even if I *was* in the middle of packing.

"We can talk about it later," I said, though I didn't know how much "later" I had. Cold sweat dripped down my temples like melting frost, and I shivered.

"I know," she said. "I'm sorry I even told you about the job when you've got your own problems. I believe you about this haunting, but it's hard to put into perspective, just something I never imagined anyone would actually get tangled up with. I hoped that moving would wipe the slate clean, all our problems taken care of. But there's always a hitch, isn't there?"

I was in fear for my life, and right now all I felt was guilt for burdening her with my woes. My eyes rolled back, and I sensed as if I was about to pass out again...

"Charlie?" Gail shook me and patted my face.

I *did* pass out.

"How long was I gone?" I asked. I sensed Rasputin's presence, but he wasn't alone. I heard Joey call to me as well: *Vkhodite.*

"Just a few minutes. You're sick, Charlie. I want to help you with all this, but you can barely stay awake. You need to go to the hospital. If what you say is true—you're infected with some sort of ghost's touch—there's no telling what hideous illness you've contracted."

"Hospitals won't help. I've got to get back and take care of this now. I'm meeting Ray at the apartments. He's got a plan."

"What's his big plan?"

I certainly didn't want to tell her we were going in there for a *stick-em-up*. "We're going to turn the record player off."

"That's it? You defeat the ghost by turning off the record player? If it's that easy, why don't I go over there and do it for you? You're too sick to do anything but sleep."

"No, Gail. You can't go in there. Hearing the music is what makes you sick."

"Wear ear plugs."

The simplicity of her declaration made me feel like a little kid being told that two pounds of turds don't fit into a one-pound box. It was too simple, too obvious, to do anything *but* make sense. Then again, nothing about those records made sense. Maybe ear plugs wouldn't work—the ghost would slip right on through the rubber. Besides that, I already heard the music in my head even when it wasn't around. But I knew, too, the closer I was in its presence, and the more I listened to Rasputin's chants, the greater effect it had on me. The ear plugs, at least, would have to slow down that effect, I presumed.

"I knew there was a reason I loved you," I said.

"What's that reason? My common sense? What about my support of your crazy ways, and my compassion and cooking and wit?"

"And extraordinary beauty," I added.

"What don't I do for you, Charlie Stewart?" She pinched the inside of my thigh.

"Stop it, I'm near an invalid!" I cried out with a giggle. The stress and fear and sickness passed for a second, just a brief moment in which the sun popped over the horizon and melted away that crushing pressure off my back. Then the sun winked out, and the pressure and fear and everything else crashed back into place.

"I've got to go," I said.

She looked at me and nodded. "I'm glad I got to see you."

"I tried calling earlier."

"I knew it was you. Sorry I didn't answer. I thought if I picked up you would cancel on dinner."

"Yeah, I was going to."

She smiled, but it was a pitiful, sad look, the expression of foreboding and acceptance that whatever was to happen would probably be for the worst. "I'll get those ear plugs for you. The neighbor's dogs have been keeping me up at night. I guess I won't be sleeping tonight anyway."

Gail went into the other room, and I tried imagining life without her. I couldn't. I knew she was right, that I'd grown dependent on her to keep me sane. She was the one constant in my life, like going to the track and knowing she was the winning bet every single race. Just being in Gail's presence relieved my worries, and the sound of her voice warmed me with joy. If I was to be taken away by Rasputin, like Joey, I had to make sure she didn't follow. I wanted Gail as uninvolved and distant as possible. I hoped she'd have the life she deserved in New York, and I knew it was a long stretch to even consider me being a part of it, given the condition I was in. I know how hokey it sounds but, regardless of what would happen, I just wanted her to be happy.

She returned into the room, and I thought of the dramatic final scenes I'd seen in movies like *Gone With the Wind* and *Casablanca*, those "good-byes" that stain your memories forever with tears. I wanted my good-bye to have meaning.

Instead, I planted my face in my hands. "Can you give me a ride back home?"

-SL-
©2020

7.

GAIL ASKED A lot of questions as we drove back to the apartments. *How was I feeling? What else did I know about ghosts? What precautions was I going to take? What if something worse happened to me? What if I couldn't turn the record player off?* Her string of inquiries didn't instill a lick of confidence in me, and the closer we got to Les Deux Oies, the less I wanted to chat about it.

Above, the moon posed full. I'd never been particularly superstitious, but I thought that boded poorly. Wasn't the night of the full moon when forces of evil were at their strongest? That was when the beasties and demons came out, those creatures written about in monster books or shown oversized on the big screen. There were thin gray clouds, too, that drifted across the sky, and it made the night even more ominous.

We arrived and pulled around to the side of the building where my Crestline sat, looking sadder than a caged dog. Gail placed her hand on my wrist.

"Be careful," she said. "Are you sure you don't want me to go in there with you or wait for you somewhere close?"

"Absolutely not. I don't want you anywhere near this building."

"I'll be too far away if something happens, if you need me. It's a twenty minute drive from my house to here. A lot can happen in twenty minutes."

"I know, but you'll be safe at your home. Wait by the phone, and I'll call you when it's over. I'll be all right for now; I'll be with Ray."

"Good luck," she said and kissed me quickly on the lips.

"Love you, dear."

"Love you, too."

And then she was gone. I stood alone in the parking lot, unsure if I would ever see her again. Hell, I was unsure if I would see the next hour.

I returned inside Les Deux Oies and walked through the lobby looking for Ray or John. The whole floor was empty, and it was silent, too. Usually there sounded the hiss of turning pipes or the echoes of tenant arguments, but now it was so quiet I could've heard a mouse yawn.

I checked my watch, and what I saw caused me to want to punch myself. It was past eleven p.m. People's lives were in peril, and I still couldn't catch up to the world. Ray said to meet him in the lobby at ten o'clock, and I wound up over an hour late. Would Ray have gone up to Joey's room without me or was he still en route? Could this whole situation already be resolved? No, no... *it* was still up there; I felt it.

I needed to make a call. I could go up to my room, but I didn't want to miss Ray if he came through the lobby. I thought about leaving a note if we passed each other, but I didn't have a pen or paper. Fortunately, a payphone stood outside on the sidewalk.

A minute later I stood under the shifting moonlight, digging in my pockets for a dime. I triumphed in that small endeavor and hoped it to be an omen for the rest of the night. I dialed the rotary for Ray's North Side consignment shop. For every ring, I felt my heart beat twice as fast. Nobody answered, and I hung up before it burst.

Where was Ray? This was not good... I wondered if I should just go back up to Joey's room now, alone. I willed myself to wait a bit longer. I returned to the lobby and sat on one of the worn couches lined in pairs against the foyer. The backrests were punctured with knife slits, and springs broke through the seat cushions. More than once in the past, I'd come across a drunk passed out here.

I tried to think up a plan of attack, but I felt dozy. My mind wandered. I imagined the building back in its glitzy hotel days; there would have been a doorman dressed to the nines welcoming you inside with a big smile, and a concierge and bellhop stumbling over themselves that they couldn't shake your hand fast enough. Once upon a time, the lights in here were like a Hollywood marquee sign, and the red carpet rolled to every room.

Of course, that was an era ago. Les Deux Oies was like anything else in life; given enough time, it had faded to become a shadow of its original self, the days of newness and vitality long gone and nearly forgotten. The apartment building was no more than a piece of second-hand junk found inside someone's piece of lost baggage. Original gold leaf along the wall trim could still be seen, though now it cracked and peeled away like the hide of a dead animal. Light bulbs and bad wiring needed replacing, the wallpaper sagged, pipes leaked, and carpet stank.

Ah, who was I kidding? I condemned the building for being decrepit, when I was in the same condition. If ever a kettle called the pot black, it was me. Les Deux Oies was a good home, like an old used shoe that, once broken in, trades its shiny gloss for comfort and familiarity. I felt like I belonged here; it was something I'd grown with over the past decade. Together we'd weathered its ups and downs and begun the final descent into crumbling obscurity.

Yet I *wanted* more... I *wanted* to belong with Gail. It had been a long time since I hoped for something better for myself. Going to New York could be for me what renovations were to Les Deux Oies: a new start. Deep down inside, though, I felt I didn't deserve it. The self-doubt gnawed at me... life was so fleeting, so *cold*. It was a mockery to imagine happiness. A voice whispered of meaning beyond what life offered...

I shuddered and got up and went outside to call Ray's shop again. I let the phone ring twenty times and was about to hang up, when someone finally answered.

"Yeah?" The voice made no effort to hide its aggravation.

"Hi, is this John?" I asked.

"What of it?"

"This is Charlie Stewart. We met at the auction."

"Oh, hey. Little late to need something, isn't it?"

"I'm looking for Ray. Is he over there?"

"Ain't seen him since yesterday. Want me to take a message?"

"Do you know where he could be? It's urgent."

"Last I heard he went to your place. Didn't he show up?"

My heart sank. I had feared this. "Yeah, he was here, but he went back to the shop."

"Nobody's been here all night."

"You sure?"

"He hasn't been here. If you need something else, spit it out. I've got inventory to complete."

Vkhodite.

The word sounded so clear that I thought John spoke it through the phone. I slammed the handset against the cradle and returned inside.

If Ray never arrived at his shop, I knew where he wound up instead. Time was running out, and I prepared myself to return; I would have to end this horror alone.

This time going up the elevator, I heard the music begin to form sooner. Its amorphous essence hummed louder as I passed the third floor, filling in the silence between each click of the conveyor's ratcheting gears. The records' range was spreading. I dug into my pocket and pulled out the ear plugs Gail had given me. With them jammed into my ears, the world fell silent.

I reached the fourth floor and got out, immediately feeling the temperature drop in the hallway. A puff of wind blew along the corridor, and I thought of how many dozens of jackets I had in my room and that I should go up there and get one.

No, I thought. *If I left now, I might not have the strength to return.* I made my way to Joey's room.

His apartment was about ten rooms down from the elevator bank. I had walked the distance a thousand times before, but never before with this sense of dread. Every footfall moved in slow motion, and the distance seemed to triple. I passed two doors that were left wide open, Joey's neighbors who walked out and never returned. As I drew closer, the air grew colder still. I reached his home and didn't bother to knock. A scrim of snow and ice bordered the doorframe, and icicles hung off the knob.

I went inside.

After all I had seen over the past week, all I experienced—the craziness, the horror, the fear—I was still taken aback at the absurd changes before me.

There was no far wall to the apartment. Instead, the room acted as a clearing and, past it, were gnarled, intertwined limbs of giant pine trees that hinted at a great span of distance beyond. The living room and the stacks of baggage and collectibles were all still there but buried under a foot or more of white snow. The gramophone sat atop a stack of luggage, like an idol upon its alter, surrounded by a ring of fire. Bands of smoke circled upward, and I saw that Joey's apartment no longer had a ceiling; it was roofed only by a shower of stars twinkling across the dead-black sky.

Ray was there, kneeling at the record player. I saw, too, Yefim and Horace Wetzel prostate before the machine. There were more—ten? fifteen?—new men, women, and children in the group, though I knew immediately Joey was not amongst them. If my heart were of glass, it would have shattered at the realization he was gone; there was no coming back from wherever he'd been taken. Joey Third had made his last gamble, and it'd been a losing hand.

Even as I mourned Joey, I registered what other changes had recently occurred. Most of the people I saw earlier in the day were also gone, or replaced, including the Scandinavians, Martin and his wife. The woman with blue hair was still there, but she was as I saw Joey last: a fleeting shadow glimpsed within Rasputin, like the image of a movie projector upon the screen. There were more records stacked by the gramophone, too, more than originally came in the suitcase.

I remembered Joey telling me in the lobby, *The second voice is different on each album...* Were there more records now because more souls had been *recorded* on each? As Vic had explained, their voices were unlocking the realms of immortality through the chants. I shuddered, wondering where that immortality would be spent.

A teenage boy with unruly hair and zits on his chin stood from the group and walked into the forest, singing like he was performing an encore at the Grand Ole Opry. The tree limbs parted as he passed and then snapped back into place as if he'd never been there.

Rasputin opened his arms to me, expecting my surrender. I stood my ground, frozen by fear as much as by the cold. The apartment door opened from behind, and an Oriental woman wearing a housedress lurched inside.

She passed me, walking through the snow to the fire, and I read the single word she mouthed on her lips. *Vkhodite.*

Rasputin smiled and said something in return. I could only guess as to his reply: *Ne zaderzhivat'sya v kholodnyy i temnyy...*

People were passing through this room as if it were a way station. He was calling them, through the music, attracting more followers that he... *what?* Consumed? Assimilated? What happened to Joey and the others, where did they go?

Another gust of wind blew across the room, and the trees rustled. In that movement, their branches parted, and I saw another clearing, another campfire, far off in the distance. People were there, and I saw the singing teenage boy sit down. Behind that were the fairy-tale castles of my dreams. It was a world *within* a world, much as I saw Joey and the blue-haired woman as people *within* people, perhaps a mirror image of the reality I used to believe or, perhaps, the echoes of another time. Rasputin was calling his followers, the Misbegottens, to action.

What had happened to the real Rasputin? What had he attempted before his death? The book about him was back up in my room, and I thought of the answers it might hold.

Rasputin still looked at me, speaking, from behind the record player and campfire. How long would it take until he comprehended I couldn't hear him, that his words held no effect while I wore the ear plugs?

I rushed forward, each footfall sinking deeper into the drifts of snow. I grabbed Ray from behind and wrestled him up, trying to haul his limp weight backward and out the room. The Oriental woman had sat behind Ray, and she blocked the return path. The campfire sparked upward, and suddenly the woman reached over and tore at my face with her nails. Her eyes were blank, and her movement was as if a reflex, such as stepping on a dead cat's paw will cause its claws to extend out.

I recoiled away from the scratching woman, and Ray slipped from my hold. I tried to lift him again but he was bigger than me, and it was difficult to navigate in the snow. He began to struggle, batting away my arms, then turned and struck me with his fist. I fell to my knees in the snow, although, with its depth, it was almost like falling to my waist. I struggled to stand, and the others around the campfire rose and moved toward me. The Oriental woman lunged again, but this time I was ready. She was skinnier than a thermometer, so I just shoved her, and she fell backward on her keister.

The others came at me but, they too, had difficulty advancing through the snowdrift. Also they moved slow and stiff, as if they had boards tied to their limbs and tried to walk across a tightrope. I could evade them one-by-one, but I didn't want to find out what would happen if they got hold of me as a group.

I scrambled out through the snowdrift, which became shallower as it sloped down to the door, until I found the icy footing of the apartment floor. I ran out the doorway into the hall, followed by a swirl of flakes billowing after me. A tenant I recognized—Mr. Landis, a widower from the fifth floor—walked toward me from the elevators, head rocking side-to-side. He was the oldest person in the building, with a face like a piece of dried fruit: wrinkled and weathered and colored like something you might find on a moldy plate. He limped by with a cane, and I prepared to bowl him over if he reached for me. But Landis just passed and shuffled into Joey's room.

I saw his lips move: *Vkhodite.*

I ran to the elevators. Again. I had run more in the past week than I had all the rest of the year added up. Leave it to a life-threatening horror to give you a real workout. I waited for the doors to open and felt that music tugging at me. Even with the ear plugs, it was still working itself into my brain. I didn't know how much longer I could fight it. Rasputin's effect was truly spreading; if sound traveled outward in equal radiance, the tenants on the third floor would be just as brainwashed as those on the fifth. After that it would move to the second and sixth... There were over a hundred people living in the building and all could soon become the Mad Monk's sacrifices.

Once the elevator arrived, I punched in "six" and rode it to my floor. I bounded out and dashed to my room. I shouldn't have expected differently, but was relieved to find everything as I left it earlier in the day, when accompanied by Yefim and Ray.

The night fell late, and starlight filtered into the room. The summer temperature sank lower than it had any right to. It tolled midnight, and I knew not if that had any bearing on Rasputin's power, but considered it another poor omen, stacking in his favor like the fact of the moon being full.

Time, time, time—it was always against me. Following Murphy's law of nature, apparently when circumstances are dire, the clock will move twice as fast. As it was, the limitations of time already seemed to crop up at the worst of circumstances to interfere with my intentions. I knew I was running even more on its bad side now and aware that Rasputin grew stronger, while I deteriorated like decaying leaves.

I had to act fast. I picked up the book of Rasputin, ready to read like my life depended on it... which it did. At this point, I didn't know how much of what had been written was fact or assumption or bald-faced lie, but I didn't have the luxury of being finicky. I had to trust every word and pray the answers popped their heads up to say howdy. There was nothing else to go on.

I opened to the dog-eared page where I had earlier left off, and tried to put myself in mind of the author, the ex-disciple of Rasputin who had once been within the mystic's clutches...

Dark whispers circulated amongst Rasputin's chief followers of which I was privy. He was said to have gained access to another realm, there to escape and grow strong, one which he froze in time, mirroring the Black Forest outside Saint Petersburg where his rituals were practiced. The Misbegottens gathered every full moon at midnight to recite Rasputin's incantations.

His followers sought life beyond death, a continuation of existence in which they believed. Otherwise, preached Rasputin, the soul simply winked out like a failed bulb once the body died. His words were persuasive, nay, magical, and those who listened were easily converted. I found myself in that belief, though a part of me—a fragment of mind still filled with the holy spirit—knew that the immortality Rasputin spoke of was not for all. Rasputin took the souls of his followers for his own use, so their bodies were nothing but shambling husks submissive to his whim. I know not how many souls Rasputin required to achieve the perpetuity he sought, if the number was predetermined or required a steady flow, such as the need for sustenance once hunger strikes.

If I hadn't experienced what I did over the past week, I would've thought this book garbage, filled with the gleeful rantings of a nutcase. Again I was struck by how the perceptions of man can change so rapidly, so *dramatically*, within such a short period of time. What else that I believed so fervently was untrue? What else was possible that I considered absurd? I was prepared to nod my head if someone came up to me and said they were the demon, Zolga, teleported from a Mars brothel. I skipped ahead in the book, and what I read next, I almost wished I hadn't.

In 1915, Rasputin acquired a gramophone, a model with no identification or manufacturer's markings. Though he had written certain words in ink to be repeated by his followers, the chants were not enough. He said that his abilities ebbed and flowed like the tides of the Baltic Sea, as those who sang his name paused during song. The human condition requires respite, which Rasputin abhorred. The gramophone, however, could play his chants forever.

Somehow, through magic or trickery, he found a new manner in which to ingurgitate the life flow of his converts. On special discs that were crafted by a shadow, Rasputin recorded the voices of his Misbegottens one-by-one. I was present at such a recording session, and at what horror I witnessed was enough to break the spell over which Rasputin had chained me. Music played in the air, but as to its source I saw none. I watched a woman sit upon her knees and chant to him perhaps a hundred times:

Vkhodite. Vkhodite. Vkhodite.

Ne zaderzhivat'sya v kholodnyy i temnyy, ho prisoyedinit'sya ko mne v svet navsegda.

Vkhodite. Vkhodite. Vkhodite.

At each recital of those words, her body paled and faded, ever-so-slightly. But it was a compound effort, so that over time she completely faded away until there existed nothing but her voice, playing continually on the gramophone. She had been 'recorded' for all of eternity. At that, Rasputin glowed a ruddy hue, such as one who has imbibed a great deal of red wine on a cold night.

I felt nauseated. A heavy sickness filled my belly and spread so that every nerve cried out until I thought I would faint again. I fought to remain conscious. It was the nightmare I had lived, watching the records take away Joey and the others. Had I known earlier what I knew now, what could I have done differently? Take the record player from Joey by force? I thought, somehow, that wouldn't have changed a thing. Once Rasputin's gramophone had been turned on, there was no shutting it off.

But Rasputin was dead... he hadn't succeeded in his quest for immortality before. How had he been defeated?

During the last eighteen months of Rasputin's life, several assassination attempts were made on him, including stabbings, explosives, and gassings. He survived them all. Finally, on December 29, 1916, a group of nobles conspired together that Rasputin must be destroyed, lest all their own lives and families fall victim to his corrupted persuasions. Led by Prince Felix Yusupov and Grand Duke Dmitri Pavlovich, Rasputin was invited to a ceremony and served cakes and red wine laced with "enough cyanide to kill ten men." Reportedly, he was not affected. Prince Yusupov then drew a revolver and shot Rasputin in the back. Bolstered by Yusupov's act, other conspirators also drew and shot Rasputin until "no less than eight bullets were fired into his torso." Still Rasputin was not affected and, further, he went on to strangle Prince Yusupov to death in front of all.

I thought sarcastically, *isn't that keen*. So of course the Mad Monk was invulnerable to most methods normally used to overcome a man. I continued:

Fortunately, Pavlovich had apparently studied Rasputin and determined a weakness. He withdrew a club carved from limestone and beat Rasputin to the ground, until the others could subdue and bind his limbs. He was gagged and wrapped in a carpet and then thrown off a bridge into the icy Neva River. Rasputin was conscious and struggling to the end. His body was recovered three days later, and the official autopsy declared the sole cause of death as drowning.

I approached Pavlovich some years later and inquired discreetly as to the club. 'Calcium carbonate,' he replied. It is the most abundant mineral found in water. Calcium, in composite, forms limestone. Though not lethal, it was an infirmity to Rasputin, an indicator of his true vulnerability:

Drowning.

I remembered reading earlier that Rasputin's siblings had died by incidents related to drowning, and he'd nearly drowned himself. Only after his rescue had he begun to portray indications of supernatural powers.

Water, somehow, intertwined with his life, and drowning was apparently the one weakness of the Mad Monk since his childhood. But how could I drown him on the fourth floor of an apartment building?

Or, perhaps, the key wasn't in Rasputin himself...

I needed tools and weapons, and I looked around my apartment. I'd never felt more vindicated of my baggage winnings than at that very moment. Anything I needed to defeat Rasputin, I knew was at hand, as if I'd been subconsciously stockpiling all these years in an effort to protect Les Deux Oies. There simply wasn't anything I *didn't* have. The challenge, of course, would be in actually locating such items stored amidst the towers of castoffs.

I began searching. I was shivering cold and getting colder still, so the first item of business was to change out of my dinner suit and into warmer clothes: two layers of pants, several wool flannels, a sailor's peacoat, and boots. I thought of the locker I had, filled with equipment that once belonged to an Everest mountaineer.

Snowshoes. I rummaged through the piles and came out with a pair made from wood and rawhide. If Joey's brainwashed neighbors still sat around the fire in drifts of snow, I could at least now easily outmaneuver them. I slung the shoes over my shoulder. The locker was also crammed with pick axes, compasses, goggles, stakes, and other unfamiliar gear that smelled of mildew and old age. A leather bag of powdered chalk hung jammed into a corner; I hesitated, then tied it to my belt by its drawstring.

I saw my prized conquistador's sword and pistol hanging on hooks above a pile of bags filled with cushions and linen. The antique pistol wouldn't be of any use, but whoever owned the sword before me had kept it oiled and sharp and in otherwise exquisite condition. I lifted it, and the sword felt good in my hand. It looked to be as lethal as anything else in the room, so I hooked the scabbard to my belt opposite the chalk bag, hoping I wouldn't need to use it.

What else... I wished the original plan had gone through, and that I'd be heading to the room alongside Ray, armed with guns. Not that I was a sharpshooter, but I'd hunted a bit as a kid in Kentucky and would have preferred going into any conflict holding a Colt .45 or Browning. As to what else I could use for a weapon, my eyes scanned the room and landed on a Louisville slugger baseball bat. As good as the sword had felt in my hand, the bat felt *natural.* I'd swung a bat a thousand times for every instance I'd touched a sword.

I realized how ridiculous I must have looked: a baseball-playing conquistador dressed to hike in the snow. But everything had a purpose. I thought of also bringing the book with me but realized there would be no time to read as I ventured downstairs. I was already heavily burdened, and anything else would be detrimental, adding to my load. I was never a quick student but hoped I remembered, and *understood*, everything I'd read in its pages.

I felt as prepared as I could be given the circumstances. I considered that, should the first part of my plan inexplicably succeed, I'd need an escape from Les Deux Oies as quick as possible. Of course I remembered the Crestline was out of commission, and escaping quick wouldn't happen without the participation of someone else. It was late in the night... who could I beseech to act as a getaway driver? Who, *besides* Gail, as I didn't want to involve her further? Could I call John at Ray's shop again? He was supposed to be there all night, but could I convince him of what had occurred? He'd think I was in my room gettin' plastered.

I pulled out the ear plugs and tried John. After thirty rings, I hung up. I called Vic, though I knew he went to bed at dusk. No answer. I even rang up my bookie. No dice there either. I considered just calling a cabbie, but decided how ridiculously unreliable they were, even more so than me.

There really wasn't much of another option available. Either I tried to hotfoot it out of here for ten miles on my tired dogs, or I got a car ride from Gail.

I reluctantly called her, and Gail answered on the first ring.

"Hello?" she said.

"It's me."

"Is it over? Are you all right?"

"No, dear, not quite." I wanted to say, *it's worse*. Instead I kept my tone even without letting the fears slip through. "It'll be over soon. I do need a favor, though."

"Anything."

"I need you to drive me away from the apartments."

"You just need a ride? That's all?"

Oh, but what a ride it will be, I thought. I asked, "How long until you could get here?"

"I'm ready to leave now, so give me twenty minutes' drive time."

"Pull up to the curb outside the front entrance and keep the engine running."

She paused. "Is there anything else I should know, Charlie?"

I evaded the question. "I'm counting on you being here in twenty minutes. I'll be waiting. If I'm not outside already, wait ten more minutes and then leave. Just get far away, all the way to New York, and don't look back."

"You're scaring me. Why don't I wait as long as it takes for you to get ready?"

"If I'm not out there in time, something will have happened. Something, that if you came looking for me, would affect you, too... the ghost of Rasputin... "

"When have you ever been on time for anything? I'm not leaving you up there."

"Please, Gail. Just do as I ask. I've got enough to worry about without fretting over your safety."

She sighed, a long and deep sound as if a wind blew

through the receiver. "Okay, Charlie. I'll be there in twenty minutes and I won't wait around much longer than that."

"Thank you. And, Gail... bring ear plugs for yourself."

"I will."

On impulse, I added, "And New York sounds like a wonderful idea."

"Are you saying you'll go with me?"

"I'm just saying what I'm saying. It's a wonderful idea. If circumstances were different I'd be there in a flash. As it is... I don't know what's going to happen tonight."

"You'll pull through. You always land on your feet. Think positive, of a new life for us."

I didn't want to think of anything but surviving the next hour. "I gotta go. If all goes to plan, I'll meet you downstairs."

"I'll see you, Charlie. I know I will. I love you."

"Love you too, Gail."

I hung up, questioning if I did the right thing. My life—my soul—were already at stake... Even if she was my only hope, should I have asked her for assistance and put her at risk as well? I pushed it out of my mind. *Stay positive*, I thought, just like Gail told me. Unfortunately, I wasn't very adept at positivity.

I looked around the room one last time, hoping to draw on an inner strength found through happy memories of days lounging on the phone with collectors, and nights opening baggage with Joey. Regardless of what was to happen, I knew that part of my life was closed; nothing would ever return to the way it was.

I left my apartment and walked slowly down the hall to the elevator bank. Each step felt planned by someone other than me, like a force pulling my legs closer to it, one-at-a-time. I entered the conveyor, and that same force brought my arm up to punch the fourth floor button. I still wore the ear plugs Gail gave me, but I imagined the music playing anyway in my mind. Already my thoughts began to jumble... was it truly my imagination or did I actually hear it? Rasputin must have realized I was less susceptible to his chants when I went in after Ray. Would he double his efforts to convert me, or did he possess other facilities with which to subdue me?

I read in Rasputin's biography that he could foretell the future... I trembled, wondering if that were true and if he waited down there prepared, knowing exactly what I intended to do. I thought that, at least, he couldn't be at the height of his power, as he was still collecting souls, still passing through the process of transition.

The elevator reached the fourth floor, and I exited, pausing outside its door. The hallway before me seemed to stretch away like a narrow cobblestone lane. Snowflakes and dead leaves swirled alongside the molding, and the apartment doors appeared as hollows cut into dense groves of trees. But it appeared, too, as a simple beige hallway, covered in cheap carpet that led to Joey's room. Again I felt that sense of two worlds overlapping each other, as if one existed within the other and bulged out, overflowing its confines.

A chrome ashtray stand squatted in the corner of the hall. I took it and placed it in the elevator entrance, so that the door could not close and the conveyor descend. I walked. The same force that seemed to pull me along since I left my room now felt more urgent, more *in control.* As I approached Joey's room, the force warmed me, and I felt a flush of confidence. I realized what propelled me forward was nothing nefarious, but instead a certain stimulus. It inspired me that what I was to attempt was for "good," if good and bad could be so easily delineated. When I heard reports of heroics performed by everyday people they often remarked that whatever occurred had gone against their normal nature; they acted on impulse. I could only hope such a noble consciousness was leading me at this time.

In moments I was there, standing outside Joey's door. I grasped the knob and my skin stuck to the frozen metal. I turned it, and tiny icicles shattered within the tumbler. The door was difficult to open as the hinges were likewise frozen, and as I pushed against it with all my might, I saw that I pushed the door into an ever-deepening drift of snow.

Vkhodite.

The bad voice came back, and my sense of noble consciousness went the way of the dinosaurs. I made enough space between the door and the snow that I could slip through.

What had once been Joey's apartment could no longer be called as such. Whereas the last time I entered, the far wall had given way to dense forests, now, too, did all the other confines of the room. I shivered in a clearing carved from woods, and in all directions the trees pressed together like interlocking fingers. The doorway I passed from stood as a singular object unattached to anything but the ground, the way a gravestone thrusts from the earth.

Rasputin and the converts were gone.

I knew I'd entered the realm the book spoke of: the land

of Black Forest, frozen in time outside Saint Petersburg. Though I felt relief at his absence, part of me panicked. I had to find the record player fast. The fire still burned in the ground ahead, though the flames were low, its strength waning from the falling snow and lack of fuel. The suitcases that had served as altar for the record player were toppled over, and a group of footprints led away through the trees. He'd led them to the original clearing, where the Misbegottens once gathered for his worship.

Though all the walls and ceiling were gone, Joey's belongings remained, half-buried under snow. To my left his dining table tilted up as if an ice wave pushed from beneath. Greasy plates had slid off and piled in a heap to one side, and I saw the remains of breakfast I had brought him earlier that morning. A full day hadn't passed since our last conversation, though it seemed a lifetime ago. Rasputin's transformation was accelerating.

To my right were heaps of Joey's baggage, tumbled in disarray, but I quickly located the leather suitcase the gramophone had come in, underneath a scrim of pale snow. Apparently nobody thought twice of it; the case numbered just one of hundreds of luggage items stored throughout the apartment. Perhaps I was wrong and it held no significance, but I wagered my life that the suitcase was the only way to contain the record player. I made my way to it and immediately began to sink to my knees in the deepening snow.

I sat down to put on the snowshoes. Never having worn them before, I lashed the shoes to my feet as best I could and was amazed that they worked better than hoped. Though my steps were awkward, I no longer sank when I walked. I made my way to the leather suitcase and broke it free from the others. With the knowledge of what I now looked for, I reexamined the handle and the strange stones lining the seams of the case. I rubbed my fingers over the texture, and they felt hard and rough, not smooth like ivory which I first assumed it to be. The slight greenish hue veining the stones confirmed my belief: *limestone*. As the book described, it was antithetical to Rasputin.

Still holding the baseball bat in one hand, I took the case in the other, and walked across the clearing, following the footprints. They entered the forest, and I pursued, pushing with effort through snarling limbs. The trees were high altitude perennials, Siberian pines and junipers, and they grew close together like clumps of grass. I thought that those who walked before me must have broken through the branches already so that I would follow a cleared path, but the limbs seemed flexible, rubbery, and they snapped back into place rather than cracking off.

After a dozen yards I looked back and could no longer see the clearing I had entered from. The forest was a world of itself, a trap where one might wander lost for eternity; there were no identifying features, and even the night sky overhead didn't make sense. Where I knew the Big Dipper and Orion constellations should be present, instead shone distant pulsing orbs, smaller than the moon but expanding and contracting like the beating of a heart. Had I not the footprints to follow, I would have no hope of finding my way through. As it was, snow still fell from the sky, and the prints were gradually fading while I watched.

I hurried onward. I wanted to run, but the snowshoes made that impossible. Instead, I made long, wide steps and trusted that I moved faster than those I pursued. I was proved correct as the footprints became deeper, fresher. Soon, I saw the first figure ahead, his back to me as he stumbled and labored to march through the snow, following at a far distance from someone else.

I still wore the ear plugs, but could imagine the converts' voices, chanting in mantra as they walked. I pushed through the tree limbs with urgency and, as I grew closer to the figure, saw he leaned precariously on a cane, struggling to keep up with the others.

Mr. Landis, the oldest tenant in Les Deux Oies.

I silently asked for forgiveness and hoped that I caused him no other harm, if there was anything left of his original self which *could* be harmed. I set the suitcase down and swung the Louisville Slugger into the back of his head. I only used half my strength, but Landis crumpled like a wet bag.

I picked up the suitcase and hurried past him. Fifty yards further, I came upon the next person, the Oriental woman wearing a housedress who had blocked me from dragging Ray out of the room. Like Landis, she had her back to me and paid no notice as I crept from behind. My first thought was to wonder how she walked through the snow in just a dress without turning into a Popsicle. I supposed that in whatever state their mind existed was part of Rasputin's spiritual transcendence, and the effects of the physical world didn't affect them. I swung the baseball bat into her skull and she fell. Whatever transcendence they experienced, they were still affected by blunt-force trauma.

In front of her was another man, blindly following in the footprints of those in front of him, like a dumb trail of ants. I felled him with the bat. The orbs in the sky pulsed brighter, and the trees thinned slightly, and the land sloped downward, so that all combined allowed me a faraway glimpse of the *other* campfire. I knew this was the axis of Rasputin's realm, that which I had glimpsed from Joey's room. The fire there roared in a geyser of flame, surrounded by scores of shadowy figures kneeling in rows. Rasputin was bringing the record player home, leading the newest converts from Les Deux Oies.

I had no other plan but to move forward, approaching sleepwalking people from behind and braining them as if I were a back-alley hood. They were so single-minded in their trek not one noticed my approach. I wasn't normally much of a slugger, but in these circumstances, I was doing all right. I probably could have stood face-to-face with them and, unless Rasputin commanded otherwise, they still wouldn't have lifted a finger to protect themselves. As it was, I preferred clonking them from behind... I didn't want to see the walking-coma faces of people I once chatted with.

I came upon two women struggling through the snow, each step sinking them to their knees, and I felled them. Rasputin either didn't know, or care, that I was toppling his victims. As long as the music played, they moved forward. Perhaps I headed into a trap and Rasputin knew I would be one of his soon enough... or, perhaps, he simply didn't expect anyone to follow him into his own world.

Ahead, I saw the record player, and my heart skipped more than a beat. Two men carried it reverently between them, stepping in tandem. Even from a distance, I saw the black disc spinning beneath the needle and could imagine its music, that horrible cacophony of instruments screeching together.

I raced as quickly to them as the snowshoes would allow.

I imagined chopping down a tree, and I hit each man in the back of the head with consecutive swings. *Thwack. Thwack.* The gramophone fell into the snow, still playing.

A knife of words slashed across my thoughts. *Stoy! Predatel!*

The alarm had sounded. I saw the figures farther up the trail turn and scuttle toward me. The ant line was broken. They were coming for me any way they could, and I knew that included the Misbegottens from the distant campfire. They moved through the drifts as if in slow motion, lifting legs comically high while trying to traverse the snow. Rasputin would be among them, and I had only fleeting moments before they arrived.

I set the suitcase next to the gramophone and opened it wide. The record seemed to spin faster on the turntable as if frantically trying to hypnotize me before I confined it. If the gramophone had legs, it would have scrambled away like a spider about to get squashed. I picked it up, and the sides of the wooden base scalded my hands. I cried out and heaved it into the empty suitcase. Normally, when a record player is jostled, the arm slides and scratches the record all to hell. Not this one. It still played fine as a dancehall juke. Steam sizzled from my burned flesh, but I ignored the pain and slammed the suitcase closed. The limestone edges lined up at the seams, and for the first time I noticed that they formed a pattern leading away from each side of the handle in a series of abstract crosses. I didn't have time to examine it.

I ran.

I ran, the way a man might run who wore clown shoes, twenty sizes too large. Retreating through the woods was no easier than advancing forward only minutes earlier. One might think the way back would be less arduous, the path having been broken in. But, instead, the tree branches now seemed sturdier, less pliable to bend out of the way, yet too tough to be broken. Indeed, they seemed almost as living creatures reaching to ensnare me with contorted fingers. I dropped the baseball bat and held the suitcase with both hands, using it as a shield in front of me to push through the forest.

Stoy! Stoy!

The voice screamed in my mind, ordering me to stop, and I slowed, feeling compelled to obey. Fortunately another part of me took over. It was a part that I—like most rational people—normally kept shackled deep down in the recesses of my persona. The part that, when you're at a bar and someone spills their drink on you, wants to leap out and throttle the drunken slob. The part that, when you're handed the bill from an auto mechanic and see you're grossly overcharged, wants to slap the deceitful swindler and stuff the bill down his throat. It was the part of me that was wild with inconsequence and once outraced a cop car and another time taunted a rabid dog.

That part of me told Rasputin to kick a turd. That part of me said to keep running.

I then felt that nothing would stop me. Rasputin's voice in my brain grew louder, but I ignored it. It repeated in severity, but I knew not to stop. It got closer, so that I felt a tingle creeping up the back of my neck, like the breath of his words tickling my skin. I knew it was only in my head, but I still turned expecting the Mad Monk to be alongside, shouting right into my ears. Though I saw pursuing figures, there was nobody immediately near. I turned back, and a branch cracked into my forehead... It wasn't me *running into* a branch; the tree limb swung across the path like pulling a car antenna sideways all the way and letting go. I clunked backward, and my feet went over my head. Flashing stars exploded, brighter than the lights twinkling in the night.

Shouts and curses and strange squeals sounded through the air. I realized I could hear again, and the ear plugs were knocked loose. But the music wasn't playing; being locked up in the suitcase was apparently enough to keep it turned off. I was comforted it wouldn't brainwash me, but maybe it didn't matter... Rasputin's voice was still in my head.

Stoy! Predatel!

I staggered back to my feet and knew Rasputin and his followers were closing in. How much farther had I to go? I lifted the suitcase back up and pushed on through the trees, wary of their limbs swaying back-and-forth the way a cobra warns before it strikes. A couple more times they took a swing, but I dodged away. My legs were heavy, and my breath erupted in irregular gasps. The pulsating orbs in the sky grew larger like frightened eyes, and the snow fell harder. It became difficult to see more than five feet in front of me, but I pushed forward, head down, concentrating on following my tracks back to the apartment door.

I strained and labored and fought my way back up the path and through the trees until, with an exhausted roar, I broke through, falling into the clearing. The campfire inside what had once been Joey's room was now nothing but smoldering gray ash, and most of the suitcases around it looked like ice sculptures. The door was still cracked open as I'd left it, although slowly vanishing under snow flurries.

To my right, the trees parted easily as fluttering curtains, almost as if they bowed to passing royalty. Rasputin emerged, calmly striding with long steps to come between me and the apartment door.

But it wasn't just Rasputin. It was Ray, *within* Rasputin, looking at me through Ray's eyes that looked at me through Rasputin's eyes.

I was a goddamned war hero, those eyes seemed to say. *Look at me now.*

Then he spoke, and the voice was unmistakably that from the records.

"*Vkhodite.*"

Rasputin snapped his fingers. I shuddered. A beat passed, and he snapped again. The corners of his lips pulled tight and the tips of his white teeth showed through. He snapped his fingers again in rhythm, as if there were a secret beat only he could hear.

"*Ya pobedit*," he said. He snapped his fingers as Ray snapped his fingers, and I figured that Rasputin took on more than just the physical characteristics of those he absorbed.

I held the suitcase up, so its handle and limestone crosses pointed at him, like a talisman. Rasputin wavered, and he screwed up his face in revulsion. The limestone was said to be antithetical to him, but I didn't know to what extent that meant. Did he simply dislike it, the way I detested cauliflower, or did limestone actually injure him? Rasputin grimaced and more of his teeth showed, then he closed his eyes and, with a shout, brought both hands down on the suitcase, knocking it from my hands. A bit of steam floated from his skin where it touched the case, but it was no more than how the record player had burned me.

Of course the suitcase fell closer to him than to me, and when Rasputin opened his eyes, I saw how much that pleased him. I wouldn't be able to grab it before he took hold of me. I wanted to slice off the smile that grew on his face, so I drew the conquistador's sword from my belt.

I swung at him the way Errol Flynn might have done, in a wide, swashbuckling arc. Being as I've never struck a sword at someone before, it shouldn't have surprised me that I missed completely. Instead of advancing, my confidence waned, and I stepped back to reappraise the situation.

Rasputin's features melted, swirling, like colors of different waxes running upon each other. The mask of Ray's face was gone, and Rasputin's own showed clearly, solidly, before that too melted and then reappeared as before, a face within a face. The new face was of a woman, and I recognized her as the gorgeous wife of the Scandinavian, Martin. She wasn't so gorgeous now, but it was her, a photograph of life existing in a false vessel.

I didn't know if he was showing off or trying to intimidate me, or some law in his world required he change form every so often. Maybe he thought I wouldn't strike a woman.

I wouldn't let niceties stop me now. I pointed the sword at him, ready to charge again. "This is for Joey."

I expected him to reply with his usual *'Vkhodite,'* but he only glared at me. What he did next tormented me more than anything else he might have said; Rasputin's face melted again, and Joey's appeared. His lips pursed together and his cheeks rose, the way they would when Joey acted mischievous. I realized I shouldn't have voiced Joey's name; all that did was give Rasputin new ideas of what to use against me.

"*Vkhodite,*" he said. There it was, the word I expected, only this time it was Joey speaking to me, and I imagined: *Come in, Charlie. It's time to come on in.*

"You're nothin' but a broken record," I said. I thrust the sword forward in a straight line—no fancy arc—and it sunk dead-center into Rasputin's chest.

After all that, the sword ended up not doing a thing to help, and I got the sense Rasputin was just toying with me. He shrugged the attack off and stood there with it sticking out of him like a third arm. I thought back to the stories I'd read of him: Rasputin had been stabbed, shot, poisoned, and none of that affected him. Why would it be any different now? Joey's face looked down at me and his head shook, like I was the one to be pitied and not him.

The trees began to open up, and I saw glimpses of people about to pass through into the clearing. I had to act now. Rasputin reached his right hand across the hilt of the sword and began to pull it out of his chest. I leapt forward and grabbed at the suitcase near his feet. Rasputin reached for me with his other hand, as I thought he would.

He couldn't grab me. Rasputin fumbled and looked at his hand as if it had betrayed him, but I knew otherwise. He wore people like a layer of clothes, and part of him took on their physical characteristics. While he maintained Joey's form, his left hand was useless as a shoe full of mud. Those broken fingers couldn't do a thing but poke at me. It was a good thing, too, because when they brushed against my neck, his fingers were colder than anything I could have imagined, as if the deepest reaches of the Arctic Ocean drained into that hand. I shudder to imagine what would have happened if it could have wrapped around my throat.

I stepped away from him, triumphant, holding the suitcase once again, though Rasputin still stood before the door, and now he brandished the sword against me. On the flipside of our circumstances, I knew a sword strike would harm me plenty. I still felt the icy touch of Rasputin's hand on my neck, and it seemed the skin where he touched turned dead from frostbite. The first of the Misbegottens pushed through the trees at the clearing, tromping high through the deep snow.

I dug my hand into the mountaineer's bag of powdered chalk I carried on my belt and came out with a handful. I didn't have any wisecracking final words to add, so I just flung the dust into Rasputin's face, aiming for his eyes.

He shook his head once, about annoyed as if a horsefly meandered past. Then something changed. His mouth unhinged, and his eyes turned even bigger than they usually appeared. Rasputin screwed up his face and shrieked like a nest of hornets had been let loose in his pants. His eyes closed tight and little wisps of smoke plumed up. He whipped the sword at me quick but, blinded, his aim was even more lopsided than my Errol Flynn swing.

Limestone *did* hurt Rasputin. Maybe not permanently, but enough to slow him down. I don't know how I remembered such a thing but chalk, after all, is simply ground-up calcium carbonate. *Powdered limestone.*

I dodged to one side and ran around him and squeezed through the apartment door. I hit that hallway sprinting, but after two steps tripped over the snowshoes I still wore and went sprawling. The carpet burn was almost as bad as the shame. I heard crashing and shouts coming from the other side of Joey's room. I frantically worked at the straps holding the snowshoes onto my feet, but my fingers were numb from the cold and everything I tried doing took twice as long as it should with half the result.

"*Stoy! Predatel!*"

The voices were muffled, but they were close. Worse, I couldn't tell if they were from Joey's room or in my head or a little of both. My sight was fading from my peripheral vision, and something felt to be pushing against my guts, and I imagined Rasputin trying to force his way inside my body.

Finally the snowshoes fell off, and I ran in a staggering bounce-off-the-wall pace until I got in the elevator. I kicked the chrome ashtray aside and, as the doors closed, I saw figures stumbling out of Joey's apartment.

That elevator ride down four floors was the longest of my life. I considered how vulnerable I'd be if caught in that narrow metal box. Already the walls seemed to close in, and snow somehow followed me inside.

Stoy! Stoy!

That was definitely in my head. I cried out for the inner strength that had rescued me before to come back, but it must have taken coffee break.

Ne zaderzhivat'sya v kholodnyy i temnyy...

I shook my head back-and-forth like a lunatic, talking to myself. "No, no, go away, you're not real."

Finally the elevator reached bottom, and I tottered out into the lobby. It appeared as an ice castle, the floor shimmering blue-and-white and the broken couches arranged as a series of thrones. I heard echoes of voices chasing me from all directions. Shadows watched and grew from the corners like packs of uneasy dogs, gathering courage to attack in number. I walked through it all, letting memory guide me along; I'd strolled through the lobby of Les Deux Oies every day for over a decade. My vision was filled with falling snow, and I felt something crackling in my brain, something else strangling my throat. I gasped and staggered and forced each leg to take a step forward. I don't know how I made it out the front entrance, but soon enough I pushed through the lobby doors into Detroit's early dawning sky.

Gail was there, waiting. A tiny part of my mind—that clock-watching sense of guilt—screamed at how late I was. Hadn't I told her twenty minutes, give or take? How had I been in Rasputin's world for so long? The sun was beginning to rise, and I knew I was hours behind what I'd said, but she had stayed. I could only imagine the worry and indecision gnawing away as she sat parked by the curb, watching the front door as each second ticked away. I knew, too, that if she hadn't waited—if she wasn't there that exact moment—I would have surrendered. I would have cried out in defeat and collapsed on the sidewalk that appeared so pale and empty like a sheet of ice.

As it was, I nearly collapsed anyway. But Gail came to me straight away, wrapping an arm around my shoulder, bearing my sagging weight, and guiding me to her car.

"Is that it? The record player?" she asked.

I had to look around for a moment before I realized I held what she was referring to.

My breaths were shallow, and I startled to hear how hoarse and slow my voice sounded. "Yes... "

"So what now?"

"The river," I said. "Detroit River. Take us over Ambassador Bridge."

My hands convulsed and fingers spasmed so that they turned into claws, but I would not let go of the suitcase. I sat down in the car seat, and my entire being screamed in relief. I wanted to close my eyes and let go, but I had to wait; this wasn't over yet. Gail drove us away.

It was about a ten-minute drive to Ambassador Bridge but, like everything, time seemed to skew, shrugging off the normal laws it should have abided by. Of all the moments it had sped past while I wasn't paying attention, this instance was the opposite; time threw me for a loop and slowed to a crawling second-by-second pace in which we drove as if the brakes were on. I could have relived my life twice over by the time we were a block down Sanford Street.

Come in, come in, the voice still whispered in my thoughts. Then: *Let me in, let me in...*

It took me a moment to realize that the voice was still speaking in Russian, yet I understood the words as if they were my native tongue.

"*Vkhodite*," I said.

And I don't remember anything else about that drive or what happened afterward on the bridge.

Historic Les Deux Oies Building, Detroit, MI.
LES DEUX OIES
LES DEUX OIES
-SL-
©2020
45981-B
Wish You Were Here!

8.

ALMOST HALF A century has passed since that night, and time and I never really reconciled. In the same way that it's betrayed me so often by skipping ahead at the most inopportune moments, time has somehow now perpetrated the most reprehensible disservice of all. I find myself old and nostalgic, wondering at its tricks, and how so many years could have slipped by so quickly.

I'm told that time is a relative concept and everyone interprets it differently. I suppose that holds true because my interpretation of time on that drive to Ambassador Bridge really *was* skewed. Gail said I didn't start speaking Russian until we were already pulling onto the Bridge. The last thing I remember was that I had spoken Russian all my life.

Gail ended up being the real hero of this account. I may have found that proverbial cork to stick back into the genie's bottle, but she was the one who actually popped it in. Without Gail, I'd be nothing but a specter in Rasputin's forest, chanting for eternity alongside Joey and Ray and the others.

She said I frightened her like nobody's business once I started chanting. She drove for about a quarter mile across the river while I looked right at her and spoke a steady stream of Russian, as if I were trying to convince her of something. I snapped the latches of the suitcase open, and she saw the gramophone moving inside, struggling like a dog locked in a cage that's too small.

That's when she pulled over.

The way Gail tells it, I put up a good fight. But like I said before, I hit like a pansy, and she beat the stuffing out of me, tearing that suitcase from my cold, curled fingers. I've even got a thin scar on my lip where she punched me with the small diamond ring I'd given her. To this day, I don't know how she knew to throw it in the river, and Gail still doesn't know either. Plain ol' woman's intuition, I guess. She closed the suitcase's latches again, just as the needle fell against a record and began to play. She took that case and heaved it with the strength of a dozen lumberjacks far over the railing and into the dark water below. It sank like an anchor, and a puff of steam billowed up.

One night a long time ago—but also a long time after that affair on the bridge—Gail woke from a bad dream and urgently confessed something that since then she's never repeated. While the record player was sailing through the air, before it drowned in the river, she heard voices singing: Terrible, chanting voices, overlaying music that sounded like out-of-tune instruments filled with rattling teeth. She said she heard Joey's voice on that record. Never mind that the words were Russian, or that they were muffled through the leather case, or that she was frantic and near screaming... she knew Joey's voice, and she *knew* it was him.

Anyway, once the suitcase went underwater, it was all over. That was Rasputin's weakness—drowning—and it translated to the record player. Gail said I then fell asleep, and I slept for three days straight. She brought me back to her house and nursed me until I woke. After I regained consciousness, she offered to take me home to Les Deux Oies, but I declined. I figured there was nothing left there of the sort of value that's truly meaningful, and I have no idea whatever became of the items in my apartment.

We're married and live in Manhattan now. I've never attended a baggage auction since the last one with Ray, in which I blew twenty bucks just because I had to bid on something. I guess that's a symptom of gambling addiction, and a sign to call it quits. Of course I knew I wouldn't attend another auction anyway, because I wouldn't be able to stomach living through the memories, standing before an auctioneer and imagining Joey next to me waving his crippled hand up in the air.

I still watch the pony races from time-to-time, and I still collect, but only one thing, and Gail keeps a tight rein on that. I maintain a collection of postcards from Detroit. Old postcards, nothing newer than 1970, and only those showing scenic locations of the city. Another stipulation of the collection is that the cards must have been postmarked and sent. Unused postcards that never served their purpose—never traveled as they should—just wouldn't do.

I used to visit antique stores, perusing for these old cards, but the first time I saw a gramophone for sale I walked out and haven't set foot in any such place again. It's easier now with the internet, and I can search online for them. I've not returned to Motor City, and all my own photographs are gone, left behind in the apartment, so each old postcard I collect is special.

A new millennium is coming, but the passage of decades does nothing to diminish the pain and sorrow of what occurred that long-ago summer. I suppose that's why I collect old Detroit postcards. Although my last week there was spent in the shadows of a nightmare, the cards hearken back to all the other good years. They feature landmarks I was familiar with and often bring rise to fond memories, like the Penobscot Building, Belle Isle Park, and Tiger Stadium. I've got countless cards showing Ambassador Bridge, and I even have one featuring a front view of Les Deux Oies. Imagine my astonishment when I read the script at the bottom of that card's backside, sharing well wishes to his grandchildren: it was signed from George R. Landis... the oldest tenant of the building.

There might even be another reason I collect old postcards. It reminds me of the views of peoples' lives I once stored in trunks and chests, glimpses into their existence. I once collected their trappings and memories in my room, keeping them alive simply by my acknowledgement and my possession. If I'd destroyed those items, it would have been as if they never existed. But I kept them around, and their stories persevered.

And isn't perseverance what immortality is all about?

I'm keeping alive my memories of Detroit through these postcards, and maybe someone will keep alive my memories after I pass.

And that gets me wondering if there might even be *another* reason I collect... was there an underlying motive I kept sent postcards? Why was I compelled to continue to save people's voices? Postcards, like photographs, like albums, are recordings of people's existence. During the time Rasputin had a hold on me, how much of my soul did he carry away? Are there bits and flakes missing, screaming somewhere for me to resurrect them through a few magic words? Does a little part of me still reside in that nightmare land and, when I die, will it return to me, or I to it?

Perhaps saving voices is a means of self-preservation.

Or, perhaps, I'm wasting too much thought worrying about it. I'm an old man without many years left. I won't let time take those while I'm not paying attention to what really matters in life.

Gail's in the next room, and I might just go in there and kiss her with my scarred lip. I might just tell her something that I've said a hundred times before, though I don't think she ever tires of hearing it...

That she's the best bid I ever won.

The End

-SL-
©2020

Author's Afterword

THE BOOK YOU hold in hand (or view onscreen) has been over seven years in the making.

Of course, it only took about four months to write, and was originally published in a timely manner in September, 2013, albeit in an altered incarnation. But it went through some, *well,* trials and tribulations through the publisher after I'd submitted the original draft back in January of that year.

No sour grapes for the past or anything, but I'm just happy to be able to present this story now unaltered, in what's known as "Author's Preferred Text," and accompanied by the incredible illustrations of artist Steve Lines, whose work I adore. I was fortunate to engage Steve's services for an earlier project, illustrating an anthology I created, *A World of Horror* (nominated for the 2018 Bram Stoker Award for best anthology of the year), and thus doubly fortunate that he was willing to work with me for a second time, being on this novella!

So, onto a bit of backstory about this book.

The original idea for this project was brilliant, and championed by friend and admired author, Gene O'Neil, to revive the concept behind the old Ace Doubles series, in which two novellas are packaged together, pairing one acclaimed author with a "gifted, new, cutting-edge writer" (as selected by the acclaimed author). A number of eminent names were opted to be involved, and one of those was Lisa Morton, who then chose me as the newbie to write my first "long work," and be published alongside her, and of which I will be forever grateful for such opportunity.

The novellas are bound in the dos-à-dos binding method, each with its own cover art (creating two books-in-one, by flipping the work over to start at either the front or the back). Seriously, these two-in-one books are historically amazing, with the old Ace Doubles regarded as instrumental in promoting the talent of such "new" writers as Isaac Asimov, Dean Koontz, Philip K. Dick, and Poul Anderson!

Again, a brilliant idea by Gene, but unfortunately a less-than-pleasing publishing execution. Sales numbers were dreary, and not enough was done in way of promotion.

There emerged some bad feelings too against the publisher over contract stipulations and demands made. My novella went through edits that I felt pressured to accept, and the publisher forced a renaming of it, which became something I never cared for: the lamentable title of *Baggage of Eternal Night*.

I don't know how many volumes were originally envisioned for the series, but they began releasing at a slower pace, and by the eighth the series had died. It was unfortunate, because I thought the project had huge potential, and many of the authors involved wrote their hearts out for it—I know I did. Eventually, even Gene got fed up with it all, deeming it had been a bad deal.

As I said at the beginning, no sour grapes from me, as it was exciting at the time to be part of something new, and to be inspired and nudged forward to reach for loftier ambitions by Lisa and Gene, and certainly for the camaraderie I came to share with many of the other authors involved, who have become friends, and who I know have their own experiences to relate.

Additionally, a personal highlight was that this novella was also nominated a finalist in 2014's International Thriller Award for Best Short Story of the year, which I'm still insanely proud of.

Such are the experiences that mold us, the favorable and the unpleasant, the victories and the disappointments, lessons learned all, and part of the capricious journey taken, that, at least by its end, one can stand at a certain destination, and look back and say they persevered, and have something they're proud of, something accomplished, which in this case for me, is this story, *Last Case at a Baggage Auction*.

Midnight cheers,

—Eric J. Guignard
Chino Hills, California
May 11, 2020

-SL-
©2020

AUTHOR'S REQUEST

DEAR READER, FAN, OR SUPPORTER,

It's a dreadful commentary that the worth of indie authors is measured by online 5-star reviews, but such is the state of current commerce.

Should you have enjoyed this book, gratitude is most appreciated by posting a brief and honest online review at Amazon.com, Goodreads.com, and/or a highly-visible blog.

With sincerest thanks,

Eric J. Guignard
Author, *Last Case at a Baggage Auction*

The Author

ERIC J. GUIGNARD is a writer and editor of dark and speculative fiction, operating from the shadowy outskirts of Los Angeles, where he also runs the small press Dark Moon Books. He's twice won the Bram Stoker Award (the highest literary award of horror fiction), been a finalist for the International Thriller Writers Award, and a multi-nominee of the Pushcart Prize.

He has over one hundred stories and non-fiction author credits appearing in publications around the world. As editor, Eric's published multiple fiction anthologies, including his most recent, *Pop the Clutch: Thrilling Tales of Rockabilly, Monsters, and Hot Rod Horror*; and *A World of Horror*, a showcase of international horror short fiction.

He currently publishes the acclaimed series of author primers created to champion modern masters of the dark and macabre, *Exploring Dark Short Fiction*. Also he curates the series, *Haunted Library of Horror Classics* with co-editor Leslie S. Klinger (SourceBooks).

His latest books are his novel *Doorways to the Deadeye* and short story collection *That Which Grows Wild: 16 Tales of Dark Fiction* (Cemetery Dance).

Outside the glamorous and jet-setting world of indie fiction, Eric's a technical writer and college professor, and he stumbles home each day to a wife, children, dogs, and a terrarium filled with mischievous beetles. Visit Eric at: www.ericjguignard.com, his blog: ericjguignard.blogspot.com, or Twitter: @ericjguignard.

THE ILLUSTRATOR

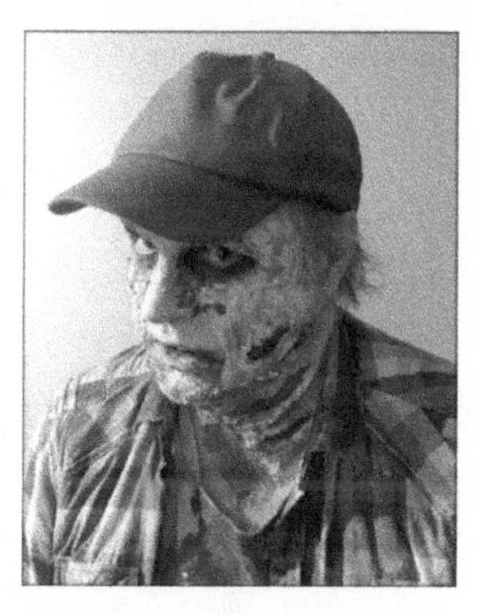

STEVE LINES is a musician, artist, editor, and occasional writer, and runs Rainfall Records & Books with John B. Ford. He lives in England in darkest Wiltshire just a few miles from the Avebury stone circle and Silbury Hill. He has been illustrating books and magazines since the mid '70s and has worked for Centipede Press, Lindisfarne Press, Mythos Books, and Rainfall Books, amongst others. With John B. Ford he wrote *The Night Eternal*, a dark Arabian fantasy. He is active in several bands including The Doctor's Pond and The Ungrateful Dead. He is currently working on a new CD album by The Ungrateful Dead titled *Dali's Brain*; putting together a new line-up of The Doctor's Pond; editing a book of sketches by Bruce Pennington; and generally keeping himself busy.

CPSIA information can be obtained
at www.ICGtesting.com
Printed in the USA
LVHW010602020920
664633LV00006B/778